For Dad
For Andrew
Mum, my best friend

And, the rest of my family, who have always encouraged
my creativeness and accepted my weirdness.

Contents

To Marry a Stranger

Chapter one

'I have just the person you need.' The skinny old man smiled at Louie and got up to shuffle around some papers. 'There's a lady who's been here since she was eleven. Orphaned. She'll be perfect for you, quiet, conscientious and does what you ask. She looks rather average but I'm assuming that won't be a problem in your circumstances.'

'Indeed Mr Jeffries. How soon can I take her?'

'When do you need her and what kind of donation will you be making to the house Mr King?'

'I need to be married within the month. The donation will depend on her education Mr Jeffries. Has she been educated?'

'Ah, yes Mr King. She went to the board school, and they were so impressed they often get her to help there now. She can read and write well and do basic arithmetic, as would be expected by such an institution.' the old man smiled proudly showing off his four and a half teeth.

Mrs. Jeffries, the matron came into the small office room. It was cramped enough with two people in there; three was almost unbearable. Louie was feeling grubby even though he had noticed that this was a relatively clean institution where everyone looked quite smart. In fact, some people in this house looked better kempt than some people who were not in the workhouse. Turning his attention back to the master, Louie had decided on a figure.

'Will one hundred pounds do well Mr Jeffries?'

The master's eyes bulged, and he rubbed his bony hands together smiling. That was more than he earned in a year. The guardians would be delighted at such a donation.

'That will do very nicely Mr King.' the master said while scribbling on another piece of paper details of the transaction. 'I will need to meet with some of the guardians, but I don't see a problem. However, we will write it on the paperwork that she is to work for you as a maid.' the master looked up and winked at Louie.

'It's pretty much true.' Said Louie handing over the money in cash. The master was taken aback as he'd never seen that much money all at the same time in actual notes. He and the matron gave each other a look of awe at this rich man that had appeared from nowhere. He spent a few moments flicking through the money, feeling it, and smelling it with a big ridiculous grin.

'Please Mrs. Jeffries would you fetch Rose?' The old man barely looked up. The matron gave a little smile and bow before disappearing back out of the door.

'May I ask sir, why you have such a small time to get married?' asked the master.

'Ugh, well, you know – families, wills...to keep my late father's house and estate.' He shrugged off the question as though it was of little importance.

'Surely you know enough beautiful ladies if I may say so sir, why don't you marry one of those?'

'No, too opinionated. They want too much. I know plenty of beautiful ladies indeed Mr Jeffries but they're only beautiful on the outside. I need someone quieter, kinder. I need someone that will look after the house and run it the way I want without question. Rest assured, she'll be well looked after.'

'Of course, Mr King, I wouldn't have thought any different.' the old man smiled.

During the short wait Louie King shuffled around the small space and watched the little man attempting to look busy but not really having anything to do. He would open a large book and shuffle through a few pages before closing it again. Then he would place another book or two on top before shuffling them around somewhere else without doing anything meaningful with them. The door re-opened, and the matron poked her head in. Thankfully, they weren't going to try to fit four people in the tiny box of a room.

'Rose is in the dining room awaiting your presence sir.' Louie thought it was quite cute how the master and matron spoke to each other. It was a very respectful manner. Louie followed Mr Jeffries to the dining hall. It was a large brick and wood room which was quite dull. The windows were so high up that he expected no one had ever cleaned them or looked out of them. What a depressing place he thought, where inmates would eat, sitting so close together they were touching the people on either side of them, with nowhere to look except at the boring beige food they were given. There were a few biblical quotes painted on the walls and on the far wall was a list of rules. There were signs indicating where the men should sit and where the women should sit.

'This is Rose Shaw, Mr King, I hope she is to your liking.' said the master, jolting Louie from his thoughts and observations. He looked at the young woman. She was looking at the floor, but he'd caught sight of her brown eyes. She had long curly dull brown hair and olive skin. His eyes did linger on her large breasts for a moment but as she looked up at him, he knew that this relationship was going to be purely a working one. She was not the type of woman he usually liked as a romantic partner, but that was fine because that wasn't what this transaction was all about anyway.

He wasn't even sure why he was feeling a small pang of disappointment.

'Would you like to come and live in a large house Rose? We'll be married and you'll do as I ask. I am a kind person though Rose.' Rose didn't answer but just shrugged and looked back at the stone floor again. Louie wondered what she was thinking, what she thought of him. Was she scared of him? Did she think he looked horrible? There were so many questions.

Before long they had arrived at Rose's new place of residence. There was a large arch gateway which led to a long winding path with trees on each side. Louie was seated opposite Rose in the carriage and watched her eyes widen as they travelled the long path to the house. He thought it strange that she hadn't said a single word since they had left the workhouse. He had kept watching her the whole trip trying to work her out, who she was and what her personality might be like. She had given literally nothing away. He was used to women talking nonstop.

As the carriage drew to a stop the cook appeared from the house doorway.

'Good afternoon, sir, have you had a good trip?'

'Yes, Elizabeth thank you. Come, I have someone to show you.' Louie couldn't help but be excited about everything when the cook was about because she always wore the most infectious smile. She'd never had children of her own and sort of adopted everyone else as her child. She bustled excitedly to the carriage where Louie was opening the door and helping the new young lady out.

'This is Rose, Rose this is Elizabeth and she's our cook.' Still Rose didn't speak and looked as though she wasn't too sure what was going on but politely smiled at the cook. Turning back to Elizabeth, Louie asked her, 'Could you find some more suitable clothes for Miss Shaw please?'

'Oh, delighted to sir.' The cook grabbed Rose's arm and took her inside the house.

Louie knew that the two women would be gone for some time. Elizabeth would be keen to show Rose every single room and heirloom while also giving the entire history of the house and everyone who'd lived there. Taking a deep breath, he decided to go to the study, as he now had a wedding to plan. The walk around the house would become boring for him anyway.

A wave of relief suddenly hit him which made him smile. Everything was going to be all right now, hopefully.

Sitting down at his desk he started to write the letters that needed to be done. One to his aunt, telling her of the impending marriage to secure his part of the inheritance, one to the reverend and one to the alehouse. Louie was most relieved about the latter as that situation was becoming quite tense. He would never be able to show his face there again, but he was fine with that.

Louie had just completed the last of the letters when his office door opened. He looked up annoyed that the person hadn't knocked, when through the door came his 'friend'.

'How did you get in Stella? Why are you here?' He asked sounding noticeably annoyed, this was the last thing he wanted right now, and he couldn't stand rudeness; especially *hers*.

'Ooh who's in a grump today?' Stella said laughing. She came over to him and sat on his lap putting her arms around his neck.

'Stella, I'm very busy today, what do you want?'

'You really are unhappy today. I just came to see my love. Come on Louie, kiss me.' she said pouting. Louie sighed loudly, still feeling annoyed about the unannounced entry. He stood up putting her on the floor and firmly removing her arms from around his neck. He really wasn't in the mood.

'You know what I've been doing today Stella, and I don't like it when you get like this.'

'Oh, is she here? Is she better looking than me?' Stella began stroking his face and attempting to rub up against him provocatively.

'No Stella, she is not better looking than you. In fact, she is quite average. Not my type. You're completely safe but you do need to stop this insecurity, we've been over this more times than I can remember. This is how it must be.' Sometimes Louie really didn't like Stella but she did have this way about her. A way of being able to physically attract him to her, and then he would end up in a cycle of having a drink, going to bed with Stella, and then regretting it in the morning when she wouldn't leave him alone again.

'Where is she, I want to see for myself.'

'I don't know, she's with Elizabeth, they're looking around the house somewhere and she is getting Rose some new clothes to wear.'

'Does she smell like pig food?' Stella laughed.

'You clearly know nothing of the workhouse Stella. She is very clean.' He hadn't realised until that moment how clean Rose had looked. 'And anyway, it's one of the better houses. Well organised. That's why I chose that one. Additionally, as I said, it's been a very busy day and I still have errands to run.'

'And a wedding to organise I suppose...' interrupted Stella.

'Yes, a wedding to organise. You need to leave, come back in a few days when you've got over whatever it is that's bothering you because I can't stand it when you talk like this – you *knew* this was happening.' Louie turned away from her and began pointlessly re-arranging things on his desk, which annoyed him more because now he felt like the old bony fingered man he'd met earlier.

'Fine, I'll go, but I'll be back, and I hope you are going to give me the attention you used to give me.'

Stella left closing the door loudly behind her. Before he'd had a chance to remove the encounter from his mind Elizabeth and Rose returned and came into the office after lightly knocking on the door.

'She's delightful sir, look at that beautiful face. Isn't she so sweet?' Louie looked from Elizabeth to Rose and back to Elizabeth.

'Has she said anything to you yet?' Louie asked.

'Not a single word sir, I think she's shy!' the cook laughed loudly squeezing Rose's arm. Louie thought sometimes she sounded a bit like a man, but she brought such happiness to the house and everyone she met. He couldn't be angry for long with her about.

'How strange.' He turned to Rose. 'I need you to sign this letter Rose and help me with some papers for the Reverend.'

Rose looked at him, shocked as if he'd just asked her to completely undress and stand on her head while holding a lit double ended candle in her mouth. He pushed the pen and papers towards her. Rose looked down at the table for a long period of time before looking up at Louie and then Elizabeth.

'You can read?' asked Louie. Rose looked down. Elizabeth took Rose's arm in her own and stroked the young girl's face.

'I don't think she can sir.'

'Rose, will you speak? Can you read, or can't you?'

Chapter two

S tella was ugly laughing hard and long, hardly able to speak. 'You're so gullible Louie! I can't believe you paid a hundred pounds and you've ended up with a grubby hornswoggler! This has got to be one of your best stupid mistakes yet.' She was laughing so much that she had to wipe away the tears that were rolling down her face.

'You're not funny Stella and SHE, is not the hornswoggler. It was the house, after all, she hasn't said a single word yet, apart from the odd yes or no here and there.'

Beginning another fit of laughter Stella said, 'it is a she? or have they fooled you there too and you're to marry a boy?'

Sometimes Louie wondered how he didn't slap Stella from one end of the room to the other. He certainly felt like it at times. In his head he apologised to his late father and mother for even having that thought. They would be mortified. Perhaps not, had they met Stella. He knew he would never really lay a finger on a woman. Even one like Stella.

'What do you want Stella? I told you not to come over until after the wedding and I thought you'd agreed. Anyway, there's nothing we can't teach her, she's a fast learner and can sign her name with no problem now.'

This made Stella laugh again.

'Well, at least she'll be able to sign the marriage certificate.'

Louie punched the desk and stood up abruptly bringing Stella's laughing fit to an equally sudden end.

'Yes Stella, and she WILL sign the marriage certificate and you will have nothing to do with it because if this doesn't go ahead, don't forget that there will be nothing. No house for a start.'

'I still don't see why you can't marry me Louie, why some strange wench from the workhouse?'

'You know we couldn't be married. We can't have a single conversation without it turning into a shouting match. We're only good for one thing Stella.'

She smiled and came over to him doing 'that thing' again.

'Well, it's a start, we can work on it.' she started kissing his neck and he didn't want her to but it was so good.

'Stella please, I'm getting married in two hours.' But she didn't stop.

'Two hours, plenty of time.' Louie gently pushed her off.

'No Stella, I need to get today right. There's a lot riding on this. Why don't you go and help Elizabeth or something if you really must hang around.'

'Yes, I must, I still haven't seen her yet. I want to see if she's spending the wedding night with you or if I am.' She laughed again leaving the room without giving Louie a chance to answer. Poor Elizabeth he thought, she didn't like Stella much at all either. It did give him a chance to get ready though.

An hour had passed and thankfully Stella hadn't returned, or he'd managed to hide well enough, he wasn't sure which. He looked around the large bedroom. It was plush with lots of patterns and puddles of fabric. Stella would hate it. It would be too bland for her, too gold and cream. Stella would want to make the room dark and plain or turn it into some kind of boudoir. They really were the complete opposite but for some reason he had spent the last hour wondering if he was doing the right thing and if he should have just married Stella like she said. He couldn't imagine living with her full time, she was just too much and so full on all of the time. He wasn't in love with her. Having said that he wasn't in love with Rose either. He sighed out loud.

There was a quiet knock at his door and to his surprise it was Rose. He gestured her into the room. She already had her dress on and looked quite pretty. She had a nice shape. The dress was a simple one but looked elegant on her despite her initial 'plain' look.

'You look very nice Rose. The dress suits you.' He said. Rose smiled.

'Why don't you say anything Rose? Are you just shy or is there some other reason?' He took her face in his hands and made her look at him. Her eyes met his and then looked down. She looked embarrassed. She was such a sweet girl that he didn't like to embarrass her. He let go and Rose sat on the chaise lounge that resided in front of the large ornate bed. Louie noticed that she sat straight and had a good posture, not slouching about like Stella did, not that Stella had been in this room. He kept this one separate; this was his special room. It had been his parents' room. When Stella was there, they used one of the other, smaller rooms. 'We must leave.' Louie said gently to Rose offering his elbow for her to take. They left together with Elizabeth and Stella for the short trip to a small chapel in the village where they would have an intimate ceremony. It wasn't what Louie had imagined his wedding day would be like, but right now it was a case of doing what needed to be done. In some ways it was a very selfish deed and he felt immense guilt for that.

The legalities completed Louie finally felt like a huge weight had been lifted from his shoulders. Although he knew the wedding was going ahead, he hadn't wanted to let himself feel completely content until it had actually happened. Anything could have happened in between.

The ceremony itself had gone smoothly, he'd managed to keep Stella away from Rose so that she couldn't say or do anything. He didn't trust Stella even after his stern warnings and explanations over the last few weeks as to why the wedding must go ahead. But now they would all be comfortable and that's all that mattered.

'That's it then, you're married to a child.' Stella said in her usual mannerism.

'What is that supposed to mean Stella, she is only four years younger than me.'

'But now you have to teach it to read and write and do all the things you thought it could do already, you have no idea how much joy I'm getting out of this Louie.'

Although he was in actual fact, painfully aware of the pure joy that Stella was getting out of this latest saga. It wouldn't even be so much of a problem if she didn't have to keep bringing it up.

Once they had returned back to the house, they found that Elizabeth had prepared an enormous lunch for everyone. An extra special one, it was still a wedding after all, and she didn't get many chances to do a big table of food. Louie wondered what time Elizabeth must have got up this morning to prepare all of this.

'Wow, Elizabeth, you've done yourself proud. What a wonderful cook you are.' Louie kissed Elizabeth on the cheek, and she squeezed his waist playfully.

'It's nothing sir, had to put on something nice for your wedding day sir.' Elizabeth looked at Stella knowing that Stella would be fuming. It was deliberate on Elizabeth's part, and she knew that Louie wouldn't even realise what was going on. It worked, that was the main thing. Stella, meanwhile, was glaring at Elizabeth and Louie. Stella had been unable to seduce Louie for at least a couple of weeks now and she was growing rather tired of it.

Stella saw an opportunity. Rose was stood alone on the far side of the table. She sidled over to make their meeting look almost accidental.

'You know you'll never be anything more than a maid. You'll have to answer to me soon because I will be the real wife. Maybe not in law. Yet. I'll make sure you see us and hear us together at every moment possible. Eventually he'll grow tired of you and put you in the asylum because there's something wrong with you!'

Rose looked at Stella making no reaction. This angered Stella more. 'Do you have any other expression? Or is that it? Well, at least we know you have no personality. He's going to get bored of you so fast.' Stella laughed turning her back to Rose and walking away. Rose looked down again feeling a small tear trying to escape her eye.

Elizabeth and Louie had both walked the length of the table but didn't see Rose wipe her eye.

'The cook, Elizabeth has suggested something to me Rose, I'd like to ask you something.' Louie said standing in front of her. Elizabeth came to the side and took Rose's arm for support.

'Elizabeth thinks that the reason you've not spoken is because you are deaf. Are you?' Louie realised that this could be rather strange, asking a deaf person if they were deaf because if they were, then how would they reply?

Rose looked at Elizabeth who smiled and nodded at her. When Rose spoke her tone was not what they expected, her words were a little slurred and unpronounced, but at last to the delight of Louie she had spoken. He was relieved as her voice was soft and gentle, not harsh like Stella. Okay, so it sounded a bit strange to begin, but he knew it would be all right.

'Not completely, just a bit. Mr Jeffries told me not to speak until after the marriage, because you'd know and might send me back.'

Louie stood back flabbergasted and speechless. In his head all he could think was, *'oh no, just wait until Stella hears this one.'* But he didn't think it was funny. He looked at Rose who was looking directly at him for the first time since they had met. He found himself wanting to help Rose. He didn't know why, but he'd decided that from tomorrow, they would begin lessons. She'd obviously had the most hideous life already, and there was no way he was going to be the one that would put her back into the workhouse, or anywhere else for that matter. The poor girl had been on her own since she was a child and by the looks of things had been virtually ignored for most of her life. Louie felt determined not to join in with the trend. The sentence that she had just spoken said so much more about her than the state of her ears. It also told him that she was honest; and that was the best asset a lady could have.

Chapter three

Rose awoke to sunlight streaming into the room and a gentle breeze blowing the curtains, so that they lapped lazily. It was so life changing to just be able to have a window open like this, and curtains - she'd never seen curtains. Yesterday had been a bit of a whirlwind but she was grateful to still be waking up in this bed and not the small hard one at the workhouse. She smiled thinking how elated she had felt once she knew that Louie wasn't going to send her back to the workhouse, or worse, the asylum. She had hugged him out of pure joy which he had reciprocated. It had felt quite nice as she hadn't had such close interaction. Life in the workhouse was all she could remember, and no contact was allowed in there. Not everyone took notice of the rules of course, but no one ever came near her because she was … different.

She walked around the room still in her night clothes, touching the fabrics and feeling the many different textures on the walls, cushions, and upholstery. The room was so clean and there was more fabric in the room than she'd ever seen. It was a dream come true for her.

Her thoughts were broken by the door opening and Elizabeth peeping in. Smiling a huge smile as usual she came into the room with a large tray containing a tea pot, a pretty little cup, toast, eggs, marmalade, milk, silver cutlery and various other little things. Rose almost couldn't take it all in. Even though she'd been here a few days now the quality and variety of food still surprised her, and it was all so colourful and tasty. Not to mention all the pretty kitchenware and heavy cutlery with intricate detailing on.

'Good morning, Rose. How are you feeling today?' Elizabeth set the tray on a table and began touching Rose's hair in awe. 'I'd love to have hair as beautiful as yours Rose.' she continued not expecting a reply to her previous question. Elizabeth had spent several hours brushing Rose's hair after washing it and it had transformed her. The wash had made it softer, and the brushing had removed a few large tangles so that now it was shiny and flowing.

Elizabeth found some new clothes for Rose and gestured her to put them on. Rose felt honoured to have so many clothes, she hadn't worn the same thing twice yet. The garments were all so much more comfortable and soft compared to what she was used to. They weren't itchy or holey and they smelled so much nicer.

Half an hour later they were walking through the large corridors with walls full of expensive paintings on the way to the drawing room where they were to meet Louie.

'Ah good morning, Rose, Elizabeth' He nodded to each in turn.

'Morning sir, I must get back to the kitchen now if it's just the same to you sir.' said Elizabeth with a little bow before leaving the room again.

Rose looked at Louie who was watching her. She felt awkward and didn't know if she should stand where she was or sit down or something. He hadn't said what he wanted, and she was unsure of the correct etiquette.

'I have to admit Rose, that I don't really know how to go about this. Er, how much can you actually hear?' He asked coming closer to her. She looked much better in the dresses but was still quite plain looking he thought, but in an intriguing kind of way. Perhaps because she didn't wear all the stuff on her face that Stella did, perhaps he just wasn't used to it.

'A little.' she said gesturing. 'I lip read'

Louie nodded still unsure how he was going to begin to go about this. He got out some paper, a pen and an inkwell and put them on a table that sat by one of the large windows which reached from the floor to the ornate ceiling. Rose watched his actions, slow and unsure. He kept looking back at her. It was the first time she had taken the chance to look at this man properly.

The dark blonde curls on his head flopped around his ears and

13

eyes elegantly and occasionally he would try to move them out of the way, only for them to flop right back where they had been. When the sun shone into his eyes the colour was amazing. It was a sort of light blue that glowed in the sun looking like the deep tropical oceans that she had once seen in a picture book. They were mesmerizing in the sunshine.

Louie gestured her over and stood behind the chair waiting for her to be seated. She'd not had a man do this before. Nervously she sat down and looked at the enormity of the blank paper staring back at her.

"Rose, I shall write a letter, then you shall copy it.' Rose thought he was talking in an odd simple kind of tone, much like you would speak to a child. She wondered why people found communication so difficult and wondered what life was like for people who could hear normally. She had been born this way and so had never known the difference. She realised it was probably also because he'd never been a teacher and had already admitted not knowing what he was doing.

The laborious process of writing the alphabet began. As she learnt each letter, she associated it with a sound.

'You've done well today Rose, let's hope you remember some of it tomorrow. We'll do more then. You'll be writing letters to people and books in no time. For now, I have to go out. You may stay in here and do as you wish, carry on writing if you like, look at some of the books in the library next door. I won't be back until late.'

'Stella?' Rose answered. She wondered what he was like to her. He always seemed so prim, she couldn't imagine him being romantic or laughing. He turned away from Rose and seemed unable to find words.

'I ... I have to go now Rose ... goodbye.' With that he went to the door and left. Rose continued to sit in the chair by the window which faced out onto the front driveway. A horse and carriage had just pulled up and she tried to see if there was anyone in it. She watched Louie appear there and look back at the window. She looked down pretending that she wasn't watching him and hoped he hadn't noticed her looking. After some muffled talking he was gone.

Rose sighed and looked over her messy writing and ink covered fingers. She was startled as Elizabeth came in.

'Rose, come and have something to eat. I have a great big pot of tea and some warm cakes!' Rose found herself smiling. She was sure she was going to put on a lot of weight with all this delightful food.

'Where does Louie go?' Rose asked Elizabeth once they were sat in the kitchen. She found it so much easier to talk normally and be herself in front of Elizabeth. Rose quickly noticed that Elizabeth only ever spoke to her in the same way she usually spoke to everyone else, nothing was simplified.

'Oh, probably the alehouse. They play a few card games or something. I don't really take much notice.' she laughed. Rose felt troubled as she was sure she'd heard him mention that there were problems at the alehouse.

'With Stella?' Why did she feel the need to keep asking about Stella, Rose thought angrily? The short, rotund cook laughed loudly.

'I should think so at some point. Heaven knows why he entertains that woman, she's no good for him.'

'Why didn't he marry her?' Rose asked. The cook leaned in closer to Rose and winked.

'Because he knows deep down that she's no good for him too.' Rose smiled. She thought about his and Stella's rather odd arrangement, and then of her own odd arrangement. She wouldn't change it for anything though.

Through the afternoon Rose showed Elizabeth her morning's work before wandering around the library and flicking through the various books. Some had pictures and some were just pages upon pages of writing and scribbles. Hours passed; she'd never seen so many books. She smelled them, she felt over the textures of the cover and the way the print stood out a little on each page. Some of the books were large and heavy, covered in fabric and gold design work. Some were small and flimsy, much less serious looking. Rose decided this was one of her favourite rooms, aside from the kitchen of course.

Outside darkness was setting in but the silence was unceremoniously broken by the slamming of the front door and the loud voices of Stella and Louie in the entrance hall. Rose stayed quiet and hoped they wouldn't come into the library where she still was. She heard them go past the door and up the stairs and she returned to picking out books and sitting on the pretty embroidered chair to flick through it. Her peace didn't last long though as a few moments later Stella crashed into the library closing the door behind her. Rose felt her legs go a bit jelly like.

'Oh, look it's the stupid fake. You know, Louie can't stand you. He said you look like a horse, but that you couldn't be a horse because a horse could write better.' Stella had sat on the arm of the chair looking down at Rose. Rose noticed that Stella's face looked ... crusty... too much make up. She was wearing bright red lipstick which was a little smudged on one side and she had too much blush, so she looked like a circus clown. She also seemed a bit wobbly and smelled strongly of alcohol.

'Oh yes, I forgot, you don't talk do you. By the way, you might be moving out soon. He ran out of money tonight and so he bet you! If he loses the bet, it's bye bye' Her voice had gone almost screechy. Rose wondered what she meant about Louie 'betting her'.

'Yes, that's right doll, but don't worry you'll be looked after exactly as you deserve ... at a hovel' Stella started to rub a finger around Rose's face.

'I bet you've never even had a smelly, sweaty man on top of you, hey Rose?' to which Stella laughed before getting up and leaving the room as abruptly as she'd entered it. Rose was left feeling completely bewildered. What had just gone on, and what did Stella mean? Rose could feel hot tears trickling down her face. Whatever the woman was talking about it sounded horrible. She liked her life here. She felt more hurt and rejected by what Louie had said about her. They had after all only done one lesson.

The house became silent, and Rose had managed to stop crying and decided to go to bed, although she wondered how she was going to sleep tonight with all those thoughts going around her head. As she walked past Louie's study she stopped momentarily.

Her heart began thumping at the thoughts she was having. She knew it was wrong.

Quietly she opened the door of the study and went inside closing it just as gently. She went to the desk not really knowing what she was going to do now that she was in here. She started shuffling through the papers on his desk. There were a lot with large letters and numbers on, and some written in red ink. She took a deep breath and decided she needed to learn how to read, and quickly. She wanted to know who this man was and why Stella had such a hold on him.

Chapter Four

'Who's a sleepy young lady this morning then?' Elizabeth laughed pulling the curtains open letting sunshine stream into the room. Rose was taken by surprise and just wanted to go back to sleep again. She felt like she'd only just managed to get to sleep and on top of that, she did not want to see Louie today. Especially if Stella was attached to him. She blinked backed tears and rubbed her eyes pretending it was a morning rub, so that the cook wouldn't realise it was because she was sad.

Elizabeth looked at her and rushed over to the bed sitting next to Rose and feeling her cheeks and head with the back of her hand.

'Are you all right Rose? You look terrible today?' Said Elizabeth. Rose laughed.

'I look terrible every day'

'Noooo! You mustn't say that you're beautiful.' With that Elizabeth enveloped Rose pulling her into her cushiony softness. Rose could feel her eyes stinging again.

'Oh Rose, whatever is the matter?' she asked wiping away the tears. 'Has that Stella said something?' Elizabeth looked stern and held Rose by the arms looking into her eyes. 'If you're upset about her don't be. She's a complete witch and should be burned at the stake to go with it!' Elizabeth pulled Rose back into her again rubbing her back and kissing her head. Rose wondered if this was what it felt like to have a ma. She began to gain confidence from the knowledge that Elizabeth was clearly her friend. She also realised that being close to Elizabeth felt very different to being close to Louie.

'Now come on' Elizabeth wiped Rose's face again. 'We have to get you up and dressed and ready for your lessons. Before that, you need a good breakfast inside you!'

Rose felt a little happier by the time she was sitting eating the large breakfast that Elizabeth had served up. Rose felt like the charming cook had made a real fuss of her this morning, and it felt genuine, she seemed to really care. The feeling was a little alien, but Rose knew one thing – it was a most pleasant feeling.

Annoyingly, just as Rose was starting to feel perkier Louie came into the dining room where they had gone for some extra tea, closely followed by the never so delightful Stella. Rose suddenly felt drained of all the lovely happy emotions she'd just had the short pleasure to experience.

'Good morning, I trust you all slept well.' Louie said to Elizabeth and Rose. They both nodded in a similar fashion after which Elizabeth found something very important to do with some plates and Rose carried on eating, staring intently at her food.

Stella joined them at the table. She put her hand on Rose's hand and gave it a little squeeze. 'Good morning Rose, you look pretty this morning, in that dress.' Rose was most suspicious of the nice tone that she had used along with the smile and apparent sudden like of her. Stella looked up at Elizabeth who was eyeing her equally as suspiciously. 'Did you pick this dress Elizabeth? It's simply beautiful, such lovely fabric and it really brings out Rose's eyes. Good choice. Don't you agree Louie?'

Rose looked around at everyone who seemed to be going through the same set of emotional and thought processes and were equally eyeing everyone else in the room. Louie looked at Stella as suspiciously as Elizabeth was.

'What?' Stella asked, trying to look innocent.

'Stop.' Louie replied.

'I'm being *nice.* You want me to stop being nice?'

'You know that's not what I meant, and neither was it what you were doing.' Rose looked down at her food again embarrassed at the exchange. Stella pulled her hand back and ate the rest of her breakfast in silence. Rose was pleased when Stella announced her departure shortly after.

Rose was keen to learn now, she wanted to be able to read the books in the library, and the strange pieces of paper strewn everywhere in the study. She was determined to concentrate and take in as much as possible today.

Rose wrote and wrote, in between attempting various words and basic reading.

'Rose, you're working hard today. I'm really impressed, you're learning so much.'

'Thank you, Louie.' Answered Rose. She looked at Louie who had started frowning at her.

'What was that you do with your hand – you always do it when you say thank you?' he asked her.

'It means thank you. It's sign language but I don't know much.'

Louie smiled. 'Oh, sign language? I'll teach you, and you teach me?' Rose smiled in return, nodding in agreement, happy that she could do something for Louie. 'Thank you.' continued Louie, repeating the same gesture that Rose had, moving his hand from his lip. Rose thought it was lovely that they had found some common ground at last and that he was happy and keen to learn, as she wasn't sure how long she would keep the hearing she did have, not that she ever remembered it being any different to how it was now.

The days became easier. Rose spent more time in the library. Many of the books in there were far too difficult to read yet at the level she was at, but she still flicked through them and picked out as many words as she could. She was also learning numbers and had learnt how to add small numbers together. Louie was going to teach her about money.

They spent a lot of time together. Often Louie would sit in the Library with Rose and read. Sometimes he would read out loud to her. She would listen intently, pacing the room or sat on the floor leaning on the chair where he was sat. Sometimes they would sit so close together that parts of their body touched, then he read quieter, more gently and she liked the feelings that she had when they touched.

During this time Rose grew ever fonder of Elizabeth and would confide everything to her. Even the little spiteful moments of Stella which Rose had learnt to ignore better. Her life would have been miserable otherwise, and Rose had a plan. A plan to make Louie proud of her.

One day in particular had stood out in Rose's mind and it was this one.

Everything had been completely normal in the morning, Elizabeth had come in as usual, Rose had got up and gone to breakfast with Louie. Stella hadn't been there in the morning on that particular day. As if it was possible, Louie and Stella seemed to have argued even more , recently.

Today Louie decided to conduct Rose's lesson in the library as she liked to spend so much time there. Rose was excited about this prospect and wondered what the morning would bring.

When she arrived at the library she was pleased to see Louie already sat at the large oval shaped table with a book in front of him. It was a large one she noticed, a very colourful one. He patted the seat next to him encouraging her to sit down.

'I thought we'd do something a little different today Rose. I thought we'd look at this book, you've not seen anything of the world. This is an Atlas and shows you about all the other places in the world and where they are in relation to everywhere else.'

It was true. She couldn't imagine life outside of the small town and local villages. She couldn't envisage that there were even other places in existence and people living their lives much like she was.

She repeated the word 'Atlas' back to Louie, it was a new word for her. She didn't know how to sign it though as she'd never had the need. She could spell it on her fingers and had taught Louie the signed alphabet so that he could sign it too.

'That's all right, we'll find out some time. Look this is where we are.' He pointed down to a minuscule piece of yellow, green rough colouring in the middle of much larger pieces of yellow, green and large swathes of blue. The writing on the page was much more ornate than what Rose was used to reading. Rose looked from the page to Louie, as he'd gone quiet, only to find him staring intently at her. It sort of, almost made her jump but not in a scary way. It was a look she hadn't seen before from him, and it had made his entire face look different. She quickly looked back to the page.

Louie cleared his throat and continued pointing out various places from the many pages of maps and getting Rose to read the place names out loud before they would sign spell them together.

'It's all right Rose, they are difficult to read with the fancy text.' he laughed, and she noticed he was watching her very closely again.

'Is there something wrong?' She asked him at last.

'No, on the contrary – what makes you think that?'

'Oh nothing.' Rose said looking back at the page and flicking to another one. 'You just keep looking at me, differently.' She said not even looking at the pages she was turning.

Louie laid his hand on top of Rose's to stop her aimlessly turning pages. She felt a strange, fuzzy, warm feeling. She didn't know what it was, but she liked it.

'I just keep waiting for you to talk like Stella or do something the way she does... and, well, you never do.' Rose thought it was probably the sincerest thing she'd ever heard him say.

At that moment Stella burst through the door. Louie quickly withdrew his hand from Rose's and Rose shuffled along the seat so that she was further away from him. His face had changed again, back to being prim and harsh.

'A... la...ska..' Rose read out loud pretending that's where they were.

'Excellent, I think that will do for today Rose. Why don't you take this one with you and see what you can find. This one was my father's so please be careful with it. Take the rest of your writing and perhaps we could do a little test in a few days. You're doing really well.' Louie smiled at Rose, but she noticed it was not how he had smiled at her just now. It was colder somehow, and he wasn't looking at her, he was looking at Stella.

Stella came and heavily placed herself on the seat between Rose and Louie even though there was room the other side of Louie. It hurt Roses leg the way she sat on it. Stella turned her back on Rose and took Louie's hands in hers. 'Hello darling, I couldn't bear to wait any longer to see you again.'

Rose felt strangely jealous but left the room carrying armfuls of books. She went to what they called the day room where there was a small piano and lots of huge windows and draped curtains.

The fire in there was already well alight and warming the room up nicely. The last few days had been especially cold.

Rose found an embroidered armchair near the fire and began looking through the Atlas again. She wasn't really reading anything, but just flicking the pages. She couldn't get that look out of her head. The one that Louie had given her in the library. She found it odd that she was thinking differently about this man as she'd never seen much in him and couldn't understand why Stella seemed to throw herself at him at every possible opportunity.

An hour or so passed and through the window she saw Louie standing aimlessly outside before a carriage drew up. Rose frowned, wondering what he was doing and why Stella wasn't with him. Before she could rationalise that thought she was disturbed by the door of the day room opening and closing.

Rose looked up excitedly thinking it was Elizabeth with the afternoon tea as it was about that time. Alas, it was in fact Stella. She was smiling that horrific smile of hers again. Rose's heart began to thump, and her legs felt like jelly again.

'Didn't I tell you? When you first came here, I told you that you'd never be anything but a maid. You came from the workhouse. Do you really think Louie is going to fall in love with your plain looks and your boring way? Your lifeless soul?'

Rose felt sad and angry at the same time. Why couldn't she stop this woman from walking all over her feelings, her heart, and every ounce of happiness she felt in the day?

Stella came closer and picked up some of the books Rose had been writing in.

'The fire is getting low Rose; did you forget you have to throw some rubbish on it to keep it going?' Stella threw the books into the fire.

'No!' Rose gasped. Stella laughed.

'Louie will never like the ungrateful poor girl that he was forced to marry so that he could pay his gambling and drinking debts off.

Wait until he finds out! You'll be thrown back into the workhouse faster than you can say A..laaa...s..kkkaaaa' she impersonated in a funny voice laughing more and snatching the atlas from Rose's hand.

'What are you going to do with that Stella?' Rose was terrified. Stella stepped closer to Rose and glared into her face. Without even blinking she threw the Atlas into the fire. Gasping again Rose quickly turned and retrieved the book from the fire, it was charred but the corner was alight.

The door opened and Elizabeth came in with the afternoon tea. Gasping she almost dropped the tray onto a nearby table and raced over to pat the burning book out with her apron scrunched up.

'I don't know what's got into the girl Elizabeth, I came in and caught her throwing all her books in the fire, then she picked this one up. Louie has just told her it belonged to his father, I told her not to and she said, 'watch me'. Louie will be devastated.'

Elizabeth looked at Rose with a disapproving look. Rose burst into tears, half because of the situation and half because of the unbearable burning sensation in her hand. She dropped the book and ran out of the room, racing up the stairs and into her bedroom locking the door. She cradled her arm that was now in the most unbearable pain she had ever known, wailing wildly, painfully and in great sadness. Her happy life here was sure to be at an end now.

Chapter five

Louie sat with his head in his hands on the edge of one of the embroidered seats, possibly the one where Rose had previously been sitting. Even though he was looking down he could see the remains of his father's book, still on the floor where it had been dropped, in his peripheral vision.

He was wondering what to do next. He was wondering why Rose had treated him like this after all he had done. Everything they had been through together in their short time. Were those nice feelings just him? He was wondering whether he should just take her back to the workhouse.

'I did warn you something like this would happen Louie. You wouldn't listen. Introducing a beggar girl to all this, it's just jealousy.' Stella unfortunately, interrupted the silence.

'Please leave Stella. I don't want you here at the moment. I need to think with a clear head.' Louie didn't look up. He was trying to decipher his own current feelings and didn't want Stella telling him how to feel or what to think. She had come over to him and knelt in front of him while he was thinking. She began to rub his legs, his thighs.

Louie quickly stood up pushing Stella away from him. More forcefully and without looking at her he repeated, 'please leave'.

Stella made a noise of disgust before getting herself off the floor. Not wanting to leave before having had the last word, she left Louie with her final word of the day. 'You *will* marry me, Louie.'

The door slammed and Louie relaxed slightly but also wondered what the previous statement was meant to mean and why she had said that.

No, he thought, he would never marry Stella. Nothing in this world would make him want to live with that level of constant drama. He just needed to work this situation out.

He picked up what was left of the book, it wasn't too bad. He flicked through and realised most of the inside was intact. Maybe he could have it re-covered. He put the book on a table and looked out of the window and began wondering how come Rose had been holding the book after it had already been in the fire, if she was trying to burn it. He couldn't work out why she had retrieved it again? Maybe guilt. Louie sighed deeply and shrugged to himself before quietly and slowly going out of the room.

Louie went to the kitchen but there was no sign of Elizabeth. Perhaps she was talking to Rose. He went to his study so that he could sit in peace. He started to sort out some of his paperwork, but his mind wasn't on it. He desperately wanted the letter from his aunt to arrive so that he could get out of the Stella situation. His mind was also flashing back to the explanations of what had happened while he had been out. He couldn't help but think that something didn't seem right.

Taking a deep inhale, he stood up having only been sat down for seconds, before returning to the kitchen. Oddly, Elizabeth still wasn't there. She was always there at this time, to finish up and close up after the day.

The house was strangely silent. He went to the large main sweeping staircase and slowly went upstairs not knowing what he was going to say to Rose.

He knocked gently on the door and waited. He couldn't hear anything inside. He was surprised when Elizabeth opened the door and gestured him to be quiet.

Quietly he and Elizabeth went into Rose's room. Rose was asleep but still fully dressed on top of the bed with clean wet rags from old linen hanging over her hand and one across her forehead. Elizabeth was keeping it wet.

He looked at Rose's face. She looked almost angelic. Her plainness was radiating a beauty that he'd never seen in the likes of Stella. Rose seemed so peaceful at that moment.

Once again Elizabeth indicated to him to be quiet. 'I've only just got her to sleep.' she whispered. Louie sat on the bed next to Rose and looked down at her. He lifted up the wet linens that were covering her hand and was shocked to see the level of burns on Rose's hand. He re-covered it and started using more cloths to drip cold water over it. He looked up at Elizabeth, feeling a little guilty. 'I don't understand how this happened. We had such a good day. Why did she get it back out of the fire?' He whispered half to himself and the other half to both Elizabeth and Rose, even though Rose was still sleeping.

Elizabeth rolled her eyes looking at Louie sternly. 'Have you ever thought that maybe she wasn't the one to throw the book into the fire to start with? Stella was there you know! You know what she can be like especially where Rose is concerned.'

Becoming temporarily still Louie tried to comprehend this thought. Yes, that would make sense, but why would Stella throw the book in to the fire to start with? He'd never before seen such evilness emanating from Stella. Was this a new thing? Had he simply not noticed before?

Louie continued putting water on Rose's hand and arm before stroking her face. He picked up one of her brown ringlets and moved it around his fingers. Her hair was soft and smelled like pretty flowers. He noticed she had strong facial features.

'She looks like an angel sleeping, don't you think Elizabeth?' The cook came closer and smiled at Louie like a proud parent.

'Yes sir, she is an angel. And I think you might be starting to like your wife.' She laughed quietly, winking, and nudging him jokingly.

'I started liking her quite a while ago.' He stopped playing with Rose's hair and looked up at Elizabeth. His face had changed. 'So why do I keep going back to Stella?'

Elizabeth gave a sarcastic half snort, half laugh. 'You're addicted to her. Addiction can be cured.' She smiled and stroked his face.

Louie thought about what Elizabeth had just said for a moment before bending down and kissing Rose gently on the cheek. Then he stood up from the bed and proceeded to kiss Elizabeth on the cheek. Giving her arms a squeeze, he said, 'Thank you, I don't know what I'd do without you sometimes. You're like a mum to me. I never knew mine, so I don't really know what having a mum is like, but I guess this might be the closest I get to feeling that.'

The cook smiled widely at such compliment. She'd never been able to have children. She pulled him in and gave him a motherly hug. 'And you're like the son I was never blessed with. You know, you and Rose have a lot in common.'

Louie went back down the stairs feeling different to how he had when he had gone up half an hour earlier. He knew he wouldn't be able to sleep tonight so he decided that this would be a good time to go to the study and make a concerted effort to sort his life out. Starting with the alehouse, and Stella.

Chapter six

L ouie had woken up in a sweat. In the short time he had been asleep he had experienced multiple nightmares about fires and the house burning down, but Rose had still been inside, among other dreams. In one of the dreams Stella was laughing in his face, she wouldn't stop, her face ugly and rancid. He sat on the side of his bed taking some deep breaths before throwing the large curtains open and washing ready for the day he had planned.

He went straight out. It was early, the sun had only just come up and he guessed he had only had about three hours sleep. Louie didn't even stop by the kitchen to tell Elizabeth, as he wasn't sure she was even up yet.

His first port of call was a couple of hours away.

Arriving at his Aunt Beatrice's large country house he realised he had forgotten how large the grounds were. His house and entire grounds could fit inside the house alone here with room to spare.

He noticed the maid was new. His aunt hadn't been very good at keeping staff. She could be quite brash and rude. On the other hand, when you needed her, she was the most loving person he had ever known. To see that facet of her personality was rare though, you had to be a special person in her life or have earned her utmost respect.

In no time he was sitting in one of the four drawing rooms. This one was green with lots of wood and plants. The enormous bay windows looked out onto a floral balcony that wouldn't look out of place in a hot country. Surrounding them were equally gigantic heavy velvet curtains in a deep green colour bordered at the top by an ornate pelmet of green velvet and gold decorations. Many of the plants had been in the room for a number of years and were huge, with expansive leaves and long, thick stems reaching up towards the light. The plush seating was covered in a variety of fabric throws and cushions which had been collected from his uncle's travels around the world when he had been a young merchant.

His aunt came in the room and looked at him unsurprised. She didn't greet him in the loving family way one might expect when they have been apart for several months.

'Well, sit down then boy.' She waved her hand towards one of the large sofas. Louie was annoyed that she still insisted on calling him 'boy' but decided he needed to let it go and keep his head in the right place to make today a successful day.

The maid came into the room with a tray. The cups and saucers jostled and clanked in the awkward silence that ensued while no one spoke. Aunt Beatrice sat in a chair opposite Louie. The chair was the same design as the sofa but was much higher and had arms. Between them the large table was being noisily filled with the items from the tea tray.

'Would you like anything else ma'am?' the maid asked putting the shiny silver tray under her arm.

'No, you may go.' aunt said gesturing her to leave. The maid bowed and went out of the room. Still, no one spoke until sometime after the door had closed behind the maid.

'So, where is she? Why didn't you bring her? I hope you didn't marry that awful Stella creature.' Louie watched his aunt pull a disgusted face at the thought of Stella, and it was at that moment he realised that he had definitely made the right decision by not marrying her. He smiled.

'No, not Stella. She is a little under the weather, and I left early and have some other errands to run, so I left her at home, in bed and very much asleep.'

'Well, what's her name? Goodness, tell me about her, this is like pulling teeth!' Her voice had gone high pitched, and she'd turned sideways on the chair, crossing her legs. Louie smiled more knowing that his aunt was just being her usual self.

'She's called Rose. She is very sweet, you would like her, aunt.'

'I think I'll be the judge of that, I don't think much of your previous choices of companion.'

'She's simple looking but has an inner beauty that radiates. She is loving and kind.' The words were so easy to find and say which surprised him almost as much as it was surprising Aunt Beatrice who turned and sat forward in her seat again.

'Hmm, well I suppose we'll see about that won't we.' Aunt was always sceptical, and Louie was not surprised that she was so sceptical of one of his women. Stella did not seem to reflect well with other people.

'I suppose that means that I will have to keep my side of the agreement then. I will pay you the money today before you leave.' Louie tried not to show how utterly ecstatic he was at hearing the previous sentence spoken.

'Aunt, I would like to ask you something. Why did my father never marry anyone else?'

Beatrice was pleased with this particular direction of conversation and changed her sitting position again, picking up her tea, clinking her cup around the saucer.

'Your father was totally devoted to your mother. When he lost her, he couldn't bear the thought of being with anyone else, even for the sake of you. He was happy to have a son and wanted to do everything possible to take care of you. He couldn't look at anyone else. They really were so much in love.' She sipped a little of the tea clinking the cup back onto the saucer. 'You're like your mother in a lot of ways you know. You have her eyes and gentle features, but you keep everything to yourself. You let people take you for granted.' Beatrice looked directly at Louie raising her eyebrows at him. 'Like that Stella thing...' She said almost as an afterthought.

Louie sat thinking about how his aunt wasn't too far different from the family pool herself and obviously didn't realise.

'I've been watching you over the last couple of years. Louie, I know losing your father so young has been difficult to cope with, but you know he would climb out of his casket if he knew what a mess you are in at the moment.' Louie was offended but sort of knew she was right. His dad had been such a hard worker. The entire family was, and he had spent the last couple of years living off that for free and having a good time. Now he was going to pay for it and wondered how much Aunt Beatrice knew. Apparently, more than he had originally thought.

'You have to stop all the drinking and gambling, and yes, I do know all about it boy, I know people you know!' Beatrice raised her eyebrows at him again. She clinked the cup and saucer back onto the table but remained sitting forward. Louie looked at her grey hair, ornately wrapped on her head. Large pearls on her tiny, floppy ear lobes and a large lacy choker necklace containing another pearl in the middle surrounded by more stones.

'Louie, make this work. Make your parents proud. Treat her like your father would like to have had time to treat your mother. Find something useful to do and stop all this hmm?' She looked at him earnestly. Louie was taken aback by the fact she had used his actual name. He found himself moving forward on his own chair and feeling a flurry of confidence. It was highly unusual for his aunt to be quite so intense. What she had said had struck a chord with him too. To treat Rose like his father would like to have had time to treat his mother. Now there was food for thought.

'I will Aunt Beatrice, I promise you. This is it now, everything I do, I will be doing for Rose.' He surprised himself again with the revelation and wondered what in the world he *was* actually going to do, but he knew that by the end of this day he would be doing all the right things to begin their new life. Suddenly he wondered about what might happen if Rose wasn't interested in giving his plan a go, especially after last night. After all, he hadn't believed Rose to begin with.

He didn't have time to dwell on such thoughts though, as the tea was finished, his inheritance was handed over and it was time for him to go and complete the next task of the day. This was one he was not looking forward to, but he knew that once it was done and out of the way everything would be perfect.

He stood outside of the alehouse staring at it for several minutes running the various scenarios through his mind before slowly approaching the back door. Louie knocked lightly and the door was quickly opened by a ragged looking man with a messy beard and long hair.

'Ah, Louie, come in.' Mr Johnson opened the door wider so that Louie could come past. Immediately inside the door was a large wooden table surrounded by mismatched wooden chairs. The table was filled with all kinds of things from bottles, plates, and cutlery to papers. The old man moved some things so that they could both sit down.

'I'll get straight to the point Mr. Johnson, I am here to completely pay off everything.' The man beamed; his eyes welled up. Louie couldn't understand why this might make the old man cry and he frowned in wonder. Mr Johnson took Louie's hand and shook it enthusiastically.

'Thank you, Mr. King, thank you so much.' said the old man still shaking his hand.

'Not a problem sir. I'm afraid I won't be in again though. I need to have a break and, well, you know, take a look at my life – sort myself out.'

Mr Johnson laughed still wiping away tears. 'That's all right Mr King, I understand. You and me both, I have a chance to look at my life too. Thank you, thank you.'

The deal was done quite quickly and before he knew it Louie was back outside. He took a few deep breaths. The weight had been lifted. He smiled with total and utter relief. He'd never thought this day would ever come. It felt SO good.

It was evening again before Louie made it back to the house and he had been looking forward to seeing Rose and planning what he might say, but he was met almost immediately by Stella.

'Ah, that's useful. Come to my study, I need to talk to you.' Louie said not accepting her touches and kisses.

'Huh! I need to speak to you too.' She replied huffily, obviously annoyed at yet another rejection.

The two went silently into the study and Louie sat himself behind the desk after seating Stella in front of the desk.

'So, you went to see my father today I hear?' Said Stella. Wow, that news travelled quickly thought Louie.

'Yes, I've paid him everything I owe. I have no need to go there again, and I have no need to see you again Stella. I'm afraid my life is changing, and you will not be part of it.'

Stella stood up smiling. Louie thought she was taking things quite well all things considered. She approached the desk and leant on it so that her face was near his, her hands were leaning on the desk and her bottom was sticking out in a rather unflattering position. 'Oh yes, I will. You see, the bill has gone up since you last looked. There's interest for a start. Then there's the weekly fee. You'll be paying me each week and I'll pass it on to father, you have no need to visit the alehouse again, but I promise you will *not* be leaving my father out of pocket!'

'No! I've paid everything I owe, that's it, we're done.' Louie could feel himself becoming hot with anger. Stella got even closer to him, so close Louie thought she looked like she only had one eye.

'Wrong! You owe *me*. You are not going to just drop me because you feel like it. We are going to carry on *exactly* as we are, and we'll have a nice family together. You'll put miss Stupid in the asylum and then you'll marry *me*.' Stella finished the sentence through gritted teeth.

Louie stood up. 'And what if I refuse?' Internally he felt immense rage at Stella and her persistent bullying of Rose.

'I will tell your wonderful, precious aunt all about the loving marriage you have with the *idiot* woman. I'll tell her how you bought her from a workhouse. It's going to be so easy to prove. I'll tell her how you've never even kissed, let alone anything else. I can see her face already, oh the shock, *the shame*.'

The two stood like bookends leaning on the table staring at each other.

'Get out Stella. Get out!' He was angry but didn't shout as he didn't want to alert Elizabeth. He was feeling cornered. He knew that even though his aunt couldn't stand Stella, she would be mortified to find out that he had literally bought Rose from a workhouse in order to get married, to get the inheritance. There was every chance she would revoke the inheritance too, which would leave him homeless and penniless.

'I'll give you until the end of the weekend. The start of next week, *we* go back to normal, and you will pay me each week as though I was your wife. When that money stops, I go to your aunt.' She stared hard at him before leaving.

Louie punched the desk so hard it hurt his hand. He slumped back down in the chair feeling his throat feel tight and his eyes starting to sting. He wanted to throw things, to break everything within his sight. He wanted to run away and start all over again. It had been such a long couple of days, and he had thought this day was going to be the start of a new life. He thought he had closed off the chapter of his more recent life that he was not so proud of, but it was far from over.

Chapter seven

'Thank you, Elizabeth.' Rose said smiling at the large tray of tea and cakes that the cook had brought up to her room.

'How's the hand feeling?'

'Much better, still a bit sore but not like it was the other night. Gosh I could have cut it off.' Both Elizabeth and Louie had learnt how to speak loud and clear enough for Rose to understand. It didn't even need to be *that* loud, just clear. They'd make sure they had her attention first so that she could lip read as well, and often find appropriate gestures with their hands. Rose really appreciated all the things they did to include her in conversations, no one else had ever done that before; she had simply just been left.

'Good. Glad to hear it. It's been five days now, so I'd be worried if it was getting worse. I'll be back up to change the dressings later.' Elizabeth got up to leave but Rose caught her apron.

'Elizabeth? Why is Stella here?' Elizabeth took Rose's hand that was on her apron.

'I have no idea. I don't know what's going on, but now he's just drinking every night. I've never seen him like this.'

'But if he's not happy, why did I see her moving so much stuff into the house yesterday?'

'I don't know. I don't know what's going on. But I promise you, I'm going to find out.'

'You and me both Elizabeth.'

Elizabeth hugged Rose. 'Drink your tea before it goes cold.' Elizabeth was smiling again before leaving the room. She'd got in the habit of locking the door so that Stella couldn't get in. A new bathroom had recently been installed in the next room which had a door leading from the bedroom that Rose was in, which made life so much easier.

Rose eagerly finished the tea and began flicking through a couple of the books that Elizabeth had brought up from the library for her to look at. One was about plants and had lots of the most beautiful illustrations, while another was about animals and also had lots of painted illustrations. She had enjoyed flicking through them, gently rubbing her hands over each page. The writing was slightly raised from the surface while the illustrations looked like they'd been coloured in right there on the page. Both were heavy books, bound in hard covers and ornate fabric and gilding.

There was a light knock at the door. That was strange thought Rose, Elizabeth didn't usually knock first, she usually unlocked the door first.

The door unlocked and Louie poked his head in. Rose stiffened feeling nervous about what he might be about to say but at the same time, delighted beyond imagination to see him. Her heart rate had almost doubled in those few seconds alone. At least it wasn't Stella, that was her worst fear.

'Good morning Rose, I wanted to come and see you.' he said closing the door and re-locking it from the inside. He walked over to the bed looking a little awkward. Louie hesitated before sitting down next to Rose, and she had shuffled over a little and moved the tray so that he could. She was trying to smile at him but knew her nerves were probably making her pull a face that was certainly not a smile.

'How is your hand?' Rose looked at the bandaged hand and back to Louie. His blue eyes had genuine concern. But Rose noticed something else, especially after having not seen him for a few days. He looked tired, drawn and almost sad. His forehead was creased where he was tense, and the whites of his eyes were pink and bloodshot from lack of sleep.

'It is much better thank you, much less painful.' Rose also noticed that his shirt was untidy and undone. He usually wore a tie and was usually very well presented but that was not how he looked at this moment.

'Good, good I'm glad it's on the mend. I was quite worried about you.' Louie looked down and changed his position slightly so that he could turn to face Rose better. Rose wanted to gather him up and tell him that whatever was bothering him was going to be all right, but that would be improper.

'I've been trying Rose...' He started before shuffling around awkwardly again. 'It's... I saw my aunt...' more shuffling and hand position changes. 'There's things you should know about me Rose.' He said all at once. Rose was feeling confused. She had been fully prepared for him to tell her that it wasn't going to work out and that he was taking her back to the workhouse. But what he was actually saying was making even less sense to her than any conversation that she had imagined might have happened. Louie sighed heavily and loudly.

'Before you came... um... well I, sometimes I played cards, you know, or we would put bets on things. Well, I erm, I spent a lot of money that I didn't really have. And then there was the drinking... and maybe a few other things.' Louie sighed loudly again. Rose didn't answer as she could tell he wanted to say more. He was looking thoughtful.

'I married you because I didn't want to marry Stella.' More shuffling. 'I owed a lot of money you see. Then there was my father who died a few months ago. Inheritance you know.' Louie looked up at the ceiling and Rose thought she saw his colour changing and his eyes looking waterier. 'a..a...anyway, a few days ago, I paid everything, you see... but...' Louie trailed off again and was shuffling and fidgeting even more. The water wells that had been filling his eyes overflowed and his cheeks became more red. 'I thought everything would be all right from there, you know...' He laid his hand on Rose's uninjured hand.

Rose was feeling quite worried. She wasn't sure where this conversation was going. In her mind she was piecing together the little pieces of life over the last few weeks that fitted in with this puzzle. Maybe that's what all those papers were on his desk that she'd seen.

'But it isn't?' she asked tentatively. Maybe he was going to say he was sending her back to the workhouse after all. She couldn't possibly go back there now, not after everything she'd been through and everything she had experienced so far in this house. She would have to beg him to let her be a maid or something. There seemed to be more tears streaming down Louie's face with each passing moment.

'She....Stella.... has put me in a position.' Sniff, shuffle. 'And I don't know what I'm going to do Rose, I don't know what I'm going to do.' Rose found herself sitting up and rubbing his arm trying to make Louie feel better but she knew that for him to be in this state, it was going to take a lot more than that.

'What do you mean Louie? Do about what?'

'Stella won't let me go Rose, she won't let us try to have a life, you see, even though it's not been that long, I've started to grow quite fond of you Rose, your beautiful soul, you're so gentle...but now I have to keep paying her and she has moved into this house. As if she is my wife. If I don't do as she demands, she will go to my aunt who could demand the inheritance back, then she could throw me out of this house. I really don't know what to do.'

Rose's mind was racing, she didn't know what to do either, but she knew she would have to think of something. Rose wished she knew Aunt Beatrice because then maybe Rose could make some suggestions. Maybe they could both go and see her and explain things.

'We'll think of something Louie, I promise we'll find a way around this. It won't be forever; we just need a plan.' She had absolutely no idea what that plan might end up being as her mind was a complete blank right now. She wanted to give him hope. For such a man to be crying here, with her, a woman he didn't really know that well, it had to be bad. Anything involving the witch Stella would have to be devastating.

'Louie, why is she doing this to you? Why you?'

'I don't know Rose, the money I owed her father at the alehouse was one of the only attachments she had over me. But once I paid it off, I thought I was free, then she changed it and said I still owe them more. I don't think I'll ever get rid of her.' The two held a long stare for some moments and Louie had begun to calm down. He put a hand on her face gently and she enjoyed feeling his warm touch, leaning into it a little. Slowly and ever so gently, they leaned into each other and embraced. He rubbed her back with his hands, and one went up to her neck under her long, bouncy hair and gently caressed her neck. The longer the hold lasted the more pleasant the feelings were.

Louie stood up looking at Rose with a look she'd never seen before. 'That was nice.' He said.

She had to lip read that time as he spoke so softly. 'I have to go now Rose, I will come back and talk to you when I can.' Louie went to the door.

'Louie?'

'Yes Rose?'

'I'm growing rather fond of you too.'

Louie smiled and left the room leaving Rose to ponder the conversation. At least she wasn't being sent away, not at the moment at least. Now she needed to think, to really think, and find a plan to get rid of Stella. Whatever the future did or didn't hold for her and Louie, Stella couldn't be part of the equation. Elizabeth had always been right about Stella. Rose still couldn't believe that such a nasty person could exist and not feel any remorse for their actions.

Rose spent the rest of the day, pacing the room, sitting by the window, and looking out before returning to the bed for a moment and pacing all over again. All the time, thinking.

Later Elizabeth came in with supper. 'Oh, Miss Rose look at you, out of bed.' she smiled, putting the large silver tray on the table by the window. 'You must be starting to feel better.'

'Yes, thank you I am..... Elizabeth?' Rose was still feeling thoughtful. Elizabeth was taking things off the tray and putting them on the table while preparing tea.

'Yes Rose? What is it?'

'I need you to do something for me.'

Chapter eight

'Tere you are sir, ma'am' Rose said with a small bow towards Stella and Louie. Louie was looking at Rose as though she was being attacked by a five headed mythical dragon as she set down their meals on the table. Rose noticed his quizzical look and gave him a quick smile and a wink while Stella was looking away.

'Back to the kitchen then girl, they don't want to look at you while they eat their breakfast.' Elizabeth said shoving Rose towards the door. Once out of ear shot, the two burst into laughter.

'Did you see his face, Elizabeth?'

'He probably thinks he's still asleep and this is some strange dream. How's the dress?'

'Perfect, thank you' And still not as itchy and uncomfortable as the ones she used to have at the workhouse.

'You have no idea how much fabric I had to take out of the waist, you need to get some meat on you!' Laughed Elizabeth patting her own rotund but homely belly.

Arriving back in the kitchen Elizabeth started giving Rose an odd look. 'What are you doing?' She asked.

Rose looked taken aback. 'I'm being a maid.' she said defensively.

'It's only meant to be for show in front of them, you don't actually have to do anything.' Elizabeth said breaking into a gigantic smile again. Rose watched her take the cutlery she had been holding before bustling about the kitchen doing what cook usually did.

'All right, I have some other ideas to explore. So I'll see you at lunch time.' Rose smiled

'I'm going to enjoy this very much.' said Elizabeth.

'Oh, me too Elizabeth. Me too.'

Rose picked up some bed linen so that it would look like she was continuing her maid duties, should she bump into Stella or Louie. There were three long flights of stairs up to the top of the house where there were several loft rooms leading off of a main corridor. No one had been up there for years, apart from when all the new bathrooms were fitted. Everything was covered in a layer of white dust. There were six good sized rooms, each with its own walk in, closet sized room off it. Each had large bay windows. Rose stood in front of one of the windows that looked over the expanse of land at the back of the house. Rose was amazed at the view. She had never seen so far all at once before. Her mouth was unconsciously open as she stood completely awestruck.

She looked back into the empty room. There was literally nothing in it apart from dust. The floorboards were bare as were the walls that looked like they hadn't been touched for years. She went to the closet area, occasionally making thoughtful noises. She explored each of the six rooms; the rooms were smaller up here but between each pair of rooms was a bathroom accessible by both rooms. Two of the rooms were filled with various pieces of old furniture which she touched and opened, exploring everything in detail.

The more she looked, the more her plan began to take shape in her mind. Smiling she crept back out onto the corridor picking up the bed linen that she had carried up and went down to the second floor. There were another six bedrooms on this floor, although one of them had recently been converted into a bathroom. This was one of the first houses in the area to have fully functioning bathrooms connected to the new sewer systems that were slowly being installed around the country. It had been a mammoth undertaking but had transformed houses such as this. It would work wonderfully for her plan too. She looked around the rooms and although these ones also hadn't been touched for quite some years, they were at least carpeted and furnished.

The first floor was where herself, Elizabeth and Louie lived. Rose knew that Louie had two bedrooms. She'd only been in his 'special' one that once, on the day of the wedding. She remembered all of the sumptuous fabrics and furniture. Her own room was by no means substandard, but his special room blew hers away. She had never been in the room that he used when Stella was there, which was pretty much all of the time now.

'Hello. Rose? Why are you in a maid uniform?' Rose turned to find herself inches away from Louie which made her gasp. He'd startled her but she had also felt a rush of something else. It was like when they had embraced the other day, but stronger. Rose looked around to make sure they were alone and then whispered as best she could.

'I have a plan, for you and me. Just trust me, and Elizabeth.' Louie looked like he couldn't make out what she'd just said or didn't understand. They were suddenly interrupted by Stella who had appeared at the top of the stairs.

'Why are you talking with the *maid* Louie? Come, we have things to do.' and with that she took his arm and dragged him away without a second look at Rose. Rose simply smiled; she was over it. She was over Stella and her stupid games. Now she was going to be playing a game of her own.

Rose went back to the kitchen. Now for the initiation of the second part of the plan.

As soon as she arrived Elizabeth beamed at her. Elizabeth's tongue was poking out between her teeth in a cheeky grin as she handed Rose a blue tablet.

'This'll do the trick.' She said.

Rose smiled in understanding as she took down a mortar and pestle from a nearby wooden shelf and began crushing the tablet. Elizabeth finished making the meals and loaded them onto the trays. Rose mixed in the now crushed blue tablet to Stella's gravy so she wouldn't notice it and they took the trays to the dining room. Rose was amazed that she managed to serve Stella's food with a completely straight and expressionless face. It would be a while before they would find out if one tablet was enough, but it should at least keep her away from Louie for the night.

Once evening approached and Rose's 'duties' were complete she retired to her room and cleared the large oak writing desk. From the drawer she obtained some thick cream coloured paper and a pen. She spent most of the night writing and drawing. Something that would continue over the next couple of weeks as she wrote out her entire plan from beginning to end. In the meantime she was hoping that Elizabeth could keep the supply of tablets up.

The next couple of weeks passed quickly, Stella seemed to believe that Rose was actually a maid although they didn't see much of her. Stella appeared to keep having some unfortunate tummy trouble, although it wasn't enough to stop her antics and so Rose with Elizabeth decided to increase the 'dose'. With pretending to be a maid and making other preparations there had been some long days. Finally though, everything was finished.

Rose was woken up by Elizabeth standing next to her with her hands on her hips looking down sternly. 'Rose! Have you not even gone to bed?' Rose looked around and sure enough she was still fully clothed and sitting at the oak desk with her head on pieces of paper sprawled all over the place.

'Oh!' she said, which made Elizabeth laugh. Not that it was difficult to make Elizabeth laugh.

'Come on we need to do breakfast!'

Rose hurried downstairs with Elizabeth, and they got the breakfasts together the same as they had every day before. When they entered the dining room, they were greeted only by Louie who seemed quite jolly and relaxed.

'Good morning, no Stella?' Elizabeth asked while noisily putting cups and pots onto the table.

'No, she was hit with a mystery illness last night, she's sleeping.'

'Oh, I hope it's nothing serious, would you like me to fetch the doctor?' Elizabeth said with such concern and sincerity that Rose thought it sounded almost genuine.

'Oh no, I'm sure it'll be fine. Just a bit of tummy trouble, that's all. Anyway, it's giving me a bit of peace.' Louie smiled. Rose dare not look at Elizabeth and busied herself with other things and arranging the curtains.

Rose wanted so much, to stay and talk with Louie but she had other plans to execute today and one of them would involve sneaking out of the house. His study overlooked the drive, in front of the house and so she needed to go while Louie was still in here. Elizabeth had a story ready if anyone should ask where Rose was so that no one would be any the wiser.

She hurriedly got changed into a more presentable dress before taking the couple of hours journey to meet Aunt Beatrice. In a bag Rose had brought with her the plans that she had been working on over the last couple of weeks. Rose had sent a letter in advance to ask if her visit would be acceptable and Elizabeth had read the letter to make sure all the spelling was correct.

Rose felt nervous arriving at the imposing house while also being amazed at the sheer size and grandeur of the place. The large front door opened, and two maids came out followed by Aunt Beatrice who stood sternly waiting to find out who the mystery wife of Louie was.

As Rose got out of the carriage, she noticed Aunt Beatrice's face soften and she might have even smiled a little.

'Hello Aunt Beatrice. It's a pleasure to meet you.' Rose said doing a little curtsey.

'Well, it's about time I saw you. Why have you come alone?' The old woman was looking closely at Rose and checking out everything from her hair to her shoes.

'Oh, Louie is ever so busy with planning...'

'Planning? What's he planning?'

'That's what I came to discuss aunt.'

'Oh, I see, well, let's go in then.'

They went to the large drawing room and Rose didn't know where to look first. There was more furniture in this one room than in her entire house. There were plants everywhere, on shelves, on the floor, hanging from the ceiling and in the windows.

Once sitting and having been served with tea and homemade scones Aunt Beatrice seemed keen to find out more about Rose.

'I'm pleased to see that you're nothing like that Stella. Awful creature.'

'Thank you, and yes, she is indeed.'

Aunt Beatrice smiled at having such agreement. She relaxed down into the chair.

'So, tell me, what's this plan you spoke of in the letter?'

'Well aunt, it begins with a large ball to open up our house....'

Chapter nine

'Did you go out today? I looked everywhere for you earlier.' Louie asked Rose, taking the moment to distract her. Elizabeth had gone back to the kitchen and Stella was still feeling unwell. He didn't want Rose to disappear out of the room again like she had this morning in a flash.

'I had an errand to run that's all.' Rose smiled.

Louie stood up and pulled Rose to him. He just couldn't stand it any longer. Every day seeing her or exchanging a few words, when all he really wanted to do was feel what he felt before, with that embrace. He thought he would never forget how that felt.

Her hands were on his chest gripping onto his jacket, and her brown eyes were wide and sparkly looking into his own. He felt that warmth again, and the nice feelings that he always had when he had any physical contact with Rose. He didn't know what he was going to do from here. He hadn't planned that moment, but the spontaneity had left him. He was however noticing new things about her face and features. He thought about when he had originally met her and thought that she looked different then. Or maybe, he just saw her differently. When they had met, he had thought that he wouldn't have looked at her twice if she had walked past him in the street or if they had met any other way. But now, he was seeing a depth to her, a deep soul that he never saw with Stella.

'You have beautiful eyes Rose, and smile. When you smile your face lights up an entire room and I.... well it was that embrace the other week... I haven't stopped thinking about it.'

At that moment they heard the door opening and jumped apart. Rose picked up the last of the items on the table and scurried out of the room while Elizabeth stood looking between Rose and Louie, who was still staring after the red cheeked Rose. Louie wondered if Elizabeth knew, or if she had seen anything.

'Is Stella no better?' Elizabeth asked smiling her infectious smile. Louie thought that if she had seen anything she wasn't showing it now.

'Yes, but still a little under the weather. I'm sure she'll be back to her usual self far too soon.' He said with an exasperated look to the ceiling.

Louie left the dining room and went to the bedroom that he was using with Stella. She was, worst luck, awake. She tapped the empty space in the bed next to her. 'Come here darling.' she said provocatively lifting a leg out of her long, silk night gown.

'Sorry Stella, I have to go out.'

Stella jumped out of bed, seeming to suddenly feel better. She came behind him and started rubbing his neck while flattening his shirt. 'Oh, come on, it's been ages.'

'No Stella.' He said moving away from her touch and finishing putting his outer jacket on.

'It's her, isn't it? The sooner we get rid of her the better.'

'We're not getting rid of her Stella, she's staying.'

'What? What do you mean she's staying?'

'Exactly that. There's no need for her to go.'

'But, all those books, the fire? She has no respect; she is jealous of you...'

'No Stella, you are jealous of her.' He said raising his voice beginning to feel frustrated and angry with Stella. 'And did she really put the books in the fire Stella? Or was it you?'

'How *dare* you.' Stella had become the brightest shade of red and was becoming angry.

'I don't know why you want to carry on this pretence Stella. We don't get on. I have nothing special to give you. You have nothing to give me. I don't understand why you don't find someone who loves you.'

'You love me, Louie.'

'No Stella, I don't.'

'You have to. You have no choice.' Stella came close to Louie and ran one of her long nails around his lips.

'I'm going out.' he repeated again, moving backwards away from her advances.

Louie left later than he had intended, feeling unashamedly regretful that she was feeling so much better already.

Once again, he found himself standing outside the alehouse. Louie became instantly confused though as it looked like it had completely shut down. Not just closed until opening time but closed closed. He looked up at the first-floor windows but couldn't see any signs of anyone there. Louie walked closer to the building and knocked on the back door. No one answered. He knocked again, but louder.

Eventually the old man opened the door. Louie thought he looked sad and more dishevelled than before. He looked as though he had lost all will.

'What do you want, it's closed.' Louie noticed that Mr Johnson's facial hair had grown even more, and he looked like he hadn't washed for some time.

'Can I come in and speak to you please Mr Johnson?' The old man eyed him suspiciously before opening the door and allowing Louie to go in. The kitchen behind the door was much the same as the last time he had visited.

'You've already paid me. I don't know what you'd want to talk to me for but let's have a drink.' said the old man pouring two glasses of ale. Louie frowned, very aware of what the man had just said but chose to not answer that at the moment. He ruminated the statement around in his head instead.

'I shut down two weeks ago. I managed to pay everything off with what you owed. That's it. We're pretty much destitute but we have a roof over our head. I still have a few debts to collect and sell a few things. What brings you here?'

'Um, well I, erm I'm not really sure if I'm honest. I wanted to ask about the bill, you know, check it was all done.' The old man laughed before taking an enormous swig from his tankard.

'Of course, it's all done. I haven't seen Stella since shutting mind.'

'She's been staying with me.'

'Oh, I see, is she well?'

'Yes, she is well.' Louie was feeling perplexed and couldn't decide whether to ask about the extra bill or whether to just bring it up with Stella later. There *was* no other bill was the crux of the matter. He realised at that moment that he was simply being blackmailed. He was starting to feel increasingly hateful towards her, but he still had no idea how to solve the problem because there was still the issue of her going to see his aunt.

Louie spent a few hours there, helping the old man out. He left some money so that Mr Johnson could buy some food and things he needed before taking his time going back home.

Once outside he looked up at the house. He couldn't bear the thought of losing his parents' house but knew he himself would have to think of something before his own money ran out; what was left of it. He briefly wondered what Rose was up to, he hadn't had a chance to speak to her about that because Stella never left his side when he was at the house.

Eventually he went inside to find Rose at the bottom of the stairs having an ankle bandaged by Elizabeth. Stella was standing nearby.

'What's been going on?' he asked sternly, looking at Stella in total distrust.

'You can't blame me this time, stupid fool fell down the stairs.' Stella screeched. Louie noticed Elizabeth shoot a look of anger at Stella and knew there had been more to it, as usual. Rose didn't say anything at all even later on the next day. He knew he would probably never find out what actually went on. Again.

Once the house was quiet, he went to the bedroom where Stella was awake and waiting for him. As he entered the door realising this, he wanted to turn around and go back out again.

'Hello lover, I thought you were never coming.' Stella said throwing back the blankets and showing him her completely naked body. Louie wished her mind and mouth matched her body as this part of her was delightful and he did miss some of the unions they had experienced. He knew he had to be very careful now. If she were to have a baby, he knew he would never be able to get away, and then he wasn't sure if he would want to live any more. He couldn't imagine a life with Stella; he would have to hide away, constantly apologising to people for her.

'I have some things to do Stella, sorry. That's what I was coming up to tell you, not to wait up.' It was already the small hours after his late trip to the alehouse.

'Why didn't you tell me you were putting on a grand ball? Half of England has been invited and I didn't even know about it!' Stella was doing her childish whiny voice again Louie thought. She covered herself back up. He had no idea what she was talking about so decided to avoid the question.

'What really happened earlier Stella? When I came back.'

'I told you earlier. So, what's the ball then?'

'I have work to do, we'll discuss it another time. Good night.' Louie said turning to go back out of the door.

'There won't be much time left! It's the day after tomorrow! How long have you been planning this behind my back?' Louie could feel himself getting angry with her, why was she so demanding? Why did she make him feel so angry all of the time? And, what in the world was this ball she was going on about?

'Good night, Stella.' He said flatly before going out of the door. As he walked down the stairs, he wondered what Stella had been talking about. The day after tomorrow would be Saturday. Confused he entered his study and sat at his desk slumping back in his chair. He focussed on a new piece of paper on his desk and picked it up. He thought it looked like Rose's writing but slightly improved.

'Grand ball, Saturday September 16th. Starting at 7pm. You don't need to do anything, it's all prepared.'

Now he was really confused. Who had prepared it and why? But the note did make him smile. In part because he knew that Rose had written it, and he was so proud of how far she had come in a short time with reading and writing and also because it must be part of whatever her and Elizabeth were up to at the moment.

He couldn't think about that for too long because he needed to work things out and see if there was a way of paying Stella enough money to make her leave him alone. He had found out the real depths of Stella's depravity after visiting her father and realising that she wasn't giving her father a penny of all the money she was scraping from him. What kind of person would live in luxury while leaving their own parent in near destitution? His thoughts turned to his own parents and how he had failed his own father in the last couple of years.

He began to wish he'd been more switched on when his father was here, listened more to him and taken his advice. He had probably assumed his father would always be there and now he wasn't. Louie felt lost. He missed his father deeply. He especially missed the moments they never had, and the things he'd never said, but should have.

Chapter ten

Elizabeth was so excited she was almost bouncing on the spot. Rose could tell she was having trouble containing herself.

'I've got something even better for tonight.' Rose didn't think it had been possible for Elizabeth to become any happier than usual, but this certainly beat it. Elizabeth waved her closed hands enticing Rose to hold her hands out with some excitable squeals. Elizabeth placed a small bottle into Rose's hands. 'Don't ask where I got it though.' She said with a wink. Rose, still confused, took a closer look at the bottle.

'Opium?' Rose said looking back at Elizabeth. Rose knew that Elizabeth did have a bit of a 'special' relationship with the doctor so she must have got them from him, thought Rose.

'She'll be out for the night. Drunk as a skunk – She won't even know her own name.' laughed Elizabeth. 'But, let me do it – we can only give her the smallest amount otherwise she won't wake up tomorrow, and while that might be a blessing, I don't really fancy prison breakfast either.'

There were lots of preparations that needed to be done for the evening which kept both Rose and Elizabeth busy for the day. Before Rose knew it dinner was done, and Stella was slumped halfway up the first staircase asking why there were rabbits jumping across the ceiling. With Elizabeth one side and Rose the other, the three finally made it to the top of the house. The dusty rooms were now clean and some of the furniture had been moved around so that all of the rooms had furniture laid out and looked homely and comfortable. Rose had been very busy putting the first part of the plan in place.

They laid Stella on the small bed. 'Perhaps we should have put her in a larger room with a bigger bed, she's going to fall off this.' Rose said.

Elizabeth stopped and looked up at Rose with an unusually serious face.

'Shame.' She said finally, which made them both burst into great laughter.

With access to the bathroom through the Jack and Gill door, the main bedroom door was locked, and they knew that they would have no trouble from Stella for the rest of the night.

'I'll keep an eye every couple of hours. Hurry up, we have to get you ready!' Elizabeth said grabbing Rose's hand to make her walk faster.

Once dressed in the most exquisite dark blue silk dress with layers upon layers of silk underskirts, Rose sat in front of the mirror so that Elizabeth could do her hair. It was so long that it took a long time to brush, but Elizabeth was very patient and spent the time telling funny stories about when Louie was younger and the things he got up to. Then she expertly plaited Rose's hair and started pinning it in various circles and patterns on her head before adding some decorations to her hair and letting a few ringlets hang gracefully down framing her face perfectly. Once finished Elizabeth stood behind Rose and put her arms around her. 'You're beautiful Rose.'

Rose held Elizabeth's arms and nestled into her. 'Thank you, Elizabeth. I don't think I could have stayed here without you; I couldn't bear it.'

Elizabeth kissed Rose's head. 'Now, enough of this, come on, you have a grand ball to host.'

Elizabeth went down the large staircases with Rose to make sure she didn't trip over any of her skirts and flowing fabrics.

A noticeable hush fell onto the large hallway as people watched Rose appear, gracefully gliding down the stairs, holding onto the oak banister with her silk gloved hand. Louie appeared at the bottom of the stairs with Aunt Beatrice. She knew she had to get straight to it before he had a chance to ask questions and before aunt gave the game away.

'Oh, my Louie, what a wonderful evening this will be, thank you so much for organising this. I'm honoured to be part of it.' Louie took her offered hand and kissed it while not once taking his eyes off of her face. Rose wondered what he was thinking right now, with his aunt next to him looking at him proudly, none the wiser and him having no idea what she would have been talking about.

'Oh, aunt, this is Rose, my wife, I don't believe you've met her yet.' Rose thought it sounded strange, Louie calling her his wife. She was, after all, his wife, but the words hadn't been spoken since that day so long ago in the chapel. Aunt Beatrice went along with it and pretended she hadn't met Rose before. There had been no prior prompting and Rose couldn't believe how easy this was so far.

'It is your ball, you must have the first dance, and the last of course but we can worry about that one later.' smiled Aunt Beatrice. Rose and Louie looked towards each other. Rose felt suddenly nervous. A dance was always an opportunity for questions to be asked.

Louie gently put one hand around Rose's waist, settling in the low, middle part of her back while softly but firmly taking her other hand in his.

Around them, people were giving applause, but Rose didn't hear it. What magic had happened she had no idea, but she felt that nice feeling that she had experienced so long ago, the last time they had embraced. There was a look in his eyes that Rose couldn't even describe. It was so far from his usual colder, business-like look that she couldn't say what it was, but it seemed loving and intense. She could feel his body under her own hands. His hand large and strong, yet gentle. Rose gazed up at his face. It looked different to how she remembered it when they met. It seemed stronger and more attractive to her.

They danced in silence for a considerable length of time. Rose was completely content and assumed that Louie felt the same. He was a very good dancer, with an excellent sense of rhythm and the ability to lead very well.

'I don't know how you managed to organise this, but it is a

wonderful evening.' He said. Rose smiled; it really was. 'Why though?' he continued.

'I wanted you to see some of the opportunities this beautiful house holds, for you, for us.' Louie momentarily stopped moving, still watching Rose. Continuing the dance Rose felt Louie pull her in closer to him with the hand on her back. They danced slower, more with each other than the music.

The quartet finished playing and again the room applauded. Music began again and now lots of people danced, oblivious to the world of Louie and Rose standing still, in the middle of the room.

Rose was feeling rather warm as their bodies were almost touching. They were so close they could still feel each other just a couple of millimetres from one another.

Another gentleman in the room came to Rose and asked to dance. The two disappeared into the crowd but Rose was still filled with all of the lovely feelings that Louie had given her. She could still see him standing in the same place, watching her. Now she just wanted to go back to him and relive that moment all over again. And again. And again.

Later in the evening Rose was kept busy, showing people around the rooms that she had cleaned and begun to organise in a way that people might like to stay there. Rose had been very careful in the process to be totally respectful of all of the belongings in the house, as she knew that a lot of it had been bought by Louie's parents and so they were all old and of sentimental value.

She had to have her business head on, but that dance had tipped her concentration. With a few stutters it did go well though and she knew that everything was going to work out. Now she just had to explain it all to Louie properly and make sure that Aunt Beatrice was still willing to help fund it to finish off some of the other rooms. Rose hoped that this would completely change the current house dynamic. She couldn't understand why Stella was still here. Not that she had to worry about her tonight. Elizabeth had kept a good eye on the old witch. She probably wouldn't be able to remember any of it by the next day.

Although Rose hadn't managed to talk much directly to Louie, she had managed to tell everyone about 'his' project for the house; the one he of course knew nothing about at this time. Throughout the night they had been close enough that Rose had been able to watch him and see how surprised he was at all the congratulations and praise for his project, and then what a wonderful wife he had too. This was perfect. But she found herself feeling other things tonight too. Things that she hadn't planned on. It didn't help that whenever she looked up, he was already looking at her across the room, in a way that she had never seen him look at her before, except maybe once, for that short time in the library.

Eventually everyone left and the house became quiet once more. The last person disappeared, and Louie closed the door leaning back onto it.

'It'll never work.' he said sadly.

'What won't?' asked Rose genuinely confused. Did he mean the business she was trying to set up or her and him, as a couple? Had he guessed the way she was beginning to think? She felt flustered and embarrassed and worried it was the latter. She had let him see a little bit of what she had been feeling and now he was going to reject her like everyone always did.

Louie walked towards her. 'We can't just open as some kind of holiday accommodation without knowing what the costs are and everything involved.' Rose felt slightly and momentarily relieved that he hadn't meant what she had thought but she was certain that it would be next.

She smiled. 'We do know. I've worked it all out.' Louie laughed and Rose looked down at the floor so she couldn't see his eyes laughing at her. That was it, he thought she was still useless and illiterate. 'Please, it's all written down, please just let me show you.' She suddenly felt silly and useless and began doubting her work.

They went to the study. Rose put a large stack of papers in front of Louie who then realised that she wasn't joking or exaggerating. He flicked quickly through, the smile gone from his face, his eyes wide and mouth agape.

'How have you learned to do all this Rose? And your writing, is beautiful.' He was rubbing his hand over some of the pages.

Rose smiled feeling more relaxed, and maybe a little flattered. He seemed awestruck.

'I suppose I had a good teacher.' She smiled. Louie looked up at her looking bashful and smiling shyly. She had meant it though. He had taught her so much in so little time.

They spent two hours talking about her ideas. Rose had worked everything out and her sums were all correct. She had made sure to check them and check them over and over again.

'There is one huge problem with your plan though Rose, and it's an amazing plan, but we could never get it off the ground, we couldn't afford it – there's just not enough money.' This was the part that Rose hadn't looked forward to. She wasn't sure how he would react to her next revelation.

'Your aunt will fund it. I spoke to her, I'm sorry I didn't ask you first.' She said quickly so that she could get all of the words out before he said anything or worse, shouted at her.

Beatrice was staying in the house tonight, in one of what would be the paying guest rooms. It was one of the ones that Rose had sorted out and Beatrice would give her verdict in the morning.

'And she agreed? I don't understand. She must have asked about the inheritance and why I don't just use that.' Louie looked concerned.

'She didn't want to know. She said it didn't matter if things were going to be sorted out. She also said she already had a fair idea what had happened to most of the inheritance anyway.'

'Really? That doesn't sound like her at all.'

'Louie, we got on really well. Don't worry, it's all good. All we have to do is work hard to get it together.' Louie was still flicking through the pages looking amazed at the writing.

Louie stood up from the desk, walking around it to stand in front of Rose who was still sitting down.

'Thank you. Thank you Rose, this is amazing, if we can make it happen. But then there's Ste...'

Rose stood up putting her index finger on his lips. 'Let's not talk about her tonight.' They remained close together, yet silent, with just the sound of the large clock in the hallway ticking.

'Dance with me again Rose.' Louie held his hand out to her and put his arm gently around her waist. Rose looked into his eyes and decided that yes, he was being serious. She placed her hand on his and he pulled her close. With one hand pressing into her back, pulling her against him, and the other holding her other hand they danced in the music of silence and ticking clocks. Rose noticed that it didn't feel odd. On the contrary. It was gentle and sensual.

Louie let go of her hand and put his arm around her back pulling her even closer to him. Tight. Then they stopped dancing and suddenly in a rush of passion Louie kissed her. The more he kissed her the more Rose wanted, and the tighter he pulled her into him, the more she wanted to be tightly pulled into him.

Chapter eleven

O pening his eyes, Louie found himself looking into Rose's eyes as she was propped up on her elbow next to him.

'How long have you been watching me sleep?' He smiled sweetly at her.

'Oh, not long. Only all night.' Rose smiled back. Louie gently stroked her face. The room had a pleasant golden glow from the early morning sun shining in the window through the curtains. Louie had taken Rose to his special room; he knew it wouldn't feel 'right' to be in the room where he and Stella usually were. Where *was* Stella? Oh well.

'It's a beautiful morning Rose, and all the better that I wake up to your beautiful soul. I've never felt so relaxed.' Mornings with Stella were always stressful. She was always telling him what she wanted of him in that day, or they would argue instantly. He would be so glad to sort out this mess once and for all. He had decided that she was no longer going to control him. Then he wondered if the thought was going to be much easier than the action. No, he must be firm, and he would be sure to take her back to her father's place himself.

'Oh Rose.' He said and started kissing her neck, face, and lips all over again.

Louie and Rose arrived at the kitchen long after Elizabeth had put away all of the breakfast food.

'Oh, good morning you two!' Elizabeth said laughing and nodding knowingly towards each. Louie noticed Rose smile shyly and go a little red. He thought that was quite sweet. As usual, the complete opposite reaction to what Stella might have had. He wondered then why he felt the need to keep comparing them, it wasn't like it was a competition. Was he really comparing them or just noticing all the things that he'd thought were normal but actually weren't? Was he realising just what a fool he'd been the last few years with Stella?

'I think Stella might have had too much to drink last night sir, found her all the way at the top of the house! Anyway, she's back in your room – she went back to bed saying she needed to sleep it off.' Elizabeth said clinking and clanking various kitchenware.

'Oh, but I didn't even see her?' Louie said confused. Elizabeth waved a dismissive hand.

'It was early on, I think. You were busy having your wonderful dance with Rose. Didn't she look the most delightful and elegant lady in the room? Apart from your aunt of course.' Elizabeth said swiftly steering the conversation away from Stella.

Now Louie was feeling shy. 'Yes, yes of course. Absolutely radiant.' He smiled remembering the sensual dances throughout the evening and the feeling of Rose in his arms.

'What will you do today Rose?' Louie asked.

'I was thinking I might carry on with those upstairs rooms and put some nice, homely things in for people.'

'Wonderful. I have some other business to attend to. I might have to go out, I'm not sure yet.' Louie knew he needed a plan. Stella wasn't going to take kindly to the total collapse of her own scheme. On the other hand, what if she went to Aunt Beatrice and then aunt withdrew the offer of funding for the business? He felt in such a difficult position and his thoughts continued in that train until he reached his study. Closing the door, the entire house felt like a different place this morning. He felt like a different person this morning. He knew he could never go back to Stella again. Not now. Not after last night.

He sat down heavily on his chair, rested his elbows on the desk and put his head in his hands. How could he get out of this predicament?

It took the entire morning of running every possible scenario through his mind before he decided to go and find Stella. He walked up the huge stairs slowly, not really wanting to do the deed, but knowing he had to, if he and Rose were to give their marriage a genuine chance. Louie stood outside the room with his hand on the door handle and his head leaning on the door frame. He took several deep breaths before going into the room.

Stella was asleep still and she looked an absolute mess, which would make things a little easier. He stood over the bed watching the woman he used to have such passionate encounters with. She was so brash and self-centred that she often didn't notice or didn't care for anything that Louie did outside of the bedroom. She didn't seem interested in *him* at all.

Stella began to wake up and Louie could feel his heart beating a little harder and faster – and not with passion! Her eyes were barely open before she was off in her usual fashion.

'I don't know what happened last night but that woman you think is so sweet and innocent is a complete witch. They locked me upstairs last night. I don't know what they gave me, but I was seeing all kinds of things. It was horrible.'

Louie had been wondering why she hadn't showed up all night. He sort of wanted to laugh but knew that would make her even more angry. 'And – the room was full of giant spiders, they kept crawling all over me.' Stella continued.

'Elizabeth said you went up there after having too much to drink. Anyway, the rooms haven't been used for some years, there's bound to be a lot of things up there.' Louie tried to steer the conversation back to some normality again and deliberately brush off her accusations. Stella was already glaring at him. He could tell she was about to have one of her outbursts which would mean he wouldn't get a word in edgeways for at least the next three hours, so he would have to get to the point, and quickly.

'Stella, I'm taking you back to your father today.' He waited and watched her face as the words began to come to realisation in her head. 'You've been blackmailing me long enough and I'm not allowing it to happen anymore. I don't really care what you tell my aunt.' He surprised himself by his matter-of-fact tone, especially considering that prior to coming into the room he hadn't been able to work out a single sentence of what to say. In his head though, he realised that it didn't matter what Stella told his aunt. Yes, he'd be devastated to lose this house, but if that was to be the cost of being rid of Stella then so be it.

'You can't! You made an agreement.' her eyes were wide; she was certainly awake now.

'I can, and I am. *You* made the agreement; I was given no choice in the matter. Things have changed a little now.' He decided to wait again. He couldn't be bothered with long explanations because that didn't work with Stella. She didn't care for explanations and rarely listened to them. She just looked flabbergasted.

'But we're made for each other Louie, you and me, that's what it's always been.' She lifted her hand and began touching his face, but Louie gently put her arm down and away from him again. She tried to kiss him, but he moved away from that too.

'Please Stella, that's not going to work now.'

Stella took a sharp breath in as though she had been given a fright. 'You... and her... Did you... Did you spend the night with her?' She sat back on the bed with a lump. Louie hoped this meant that she had realised that it was over. What a wonderful thought, for her to finally realise he didn't want her.

'I can't believe you're doing this to me. *And with HER!*' She had begun to shout; he knew that it was coming and was surprised it had taken her so long. She even managed to squeeze a couple of tears out, or maybe there were some actual feelings in there somewhere, although they weren't for Louie, and he was well aware of that now.

'But we love each other.' She whispered. It was finally sinking in. Louie couldn't believe it.

'But not, in that way Stella. You know that, come on. You love the house, my money. You want to be lady of the manor, except it wouldn't be a manor, it would be a giant drinking and gambling house and that's not where I want my life to go. I'll give you the day to get ready, I have some work to do. Then I'll take you later on, this evening. Your dad will be pleased, he's lonely Stella and you've been neglecting him. You haven't even given him any of the money I've given you. When I went to him the other day he was half starved, poor man.'

Stella looked down and turned away from Louie. Hopefully that meant she was actually feeling bad for leaving her dad like that he thought.

'What did you go and see him for, I told you not to go there.' she said quietly realising she'd been found out.

'I wanted to know about the bill Stella. The one I've already paid.'

Louie turned and left the room looking back at Stella once at the door. She didn't look up. As he walked back down the stairs, he had a sense of relief and yet a strange sadness that this particular chapter of his life was coming to an end. Those thoughts didn't last long. At the bottom of the stairs Rose had stopped, about to come up the stairs on the same side.

Louie continued down to her at the bottom step feeling unable to stay away from Rose. He wanted to be with her all day and all night. Now he knew Stella wasn't going to be in the way, that feeling was further increased. Smoothly as he reached the stair that she was on, he slipped a hand around her waist and turned her so that her back was on the decorative oak balustrade before moving close to her. Louie looked into Rose's eyes for a while, stroking her hair before kissing her gently and fully on the lips. The kisses became more passionate, and he realised that it would be a while before he got as far as his study.

Chapter twelve

Rose couldn't take the smile off her face as she looked out of the carriage while it bounced uncontrollably on the rough road they had to take to get to Aunt Beatrice's gigantic house.

The late afternoon sun was setting behind the distant trees and the evenings were starting to feel colder. Some of the trees were beginning to lose their leaves and things were turning the most amazing colours. The kaleidoscope made her feel warm despite the cold bite to the wind. Her thoughts turned to the earlier part of the day, and the last couple of days. Everything had changed so much and in a way she never would have believed possible.

Even thinking about Louie and the way he looked at her made her feel funny inside and she would have to catch her breath. As much as she tried not to let the negative thoughts in, they came anyway. Louie had explained to Rose that he was going to take Stella back to live with her father, but she dared not believe it until it happened. She began to imagine what it might be like to live in a house with her husband, acting like man and wife and without the interruptions of Stella. She never imagined that their marriage of convenience would ever become a marriage of love. Then she snapped herself out of such thoughts. She was plain old Rose Shaw, now Mrs Rose King. As if she could ever deserve such happiness – surely that was only in those books in the house library. What if he got to know her and didn't really like her that much? Everything would have changed too much at that point and her soul would be completely lost if it were to change back to how it was before she came here.

That lifetime seemed like it wasn't even hers. Each day getting up from an uncomfortable bed and dressing in uncomfortable clothes, eating breakfast often before the sun was up and then beginning work. Sometimes she would go to the school room but was always ignored because of her hearing and speech problems. It was a lonely life, but she was used to it. Hardly anyone had spoken to her at the workhouse, especially when she was a child. She'd always felt like the invisible child because none of the others ever wanted to spend time with her. So, having Louie so close and wanting to spend time with her was the most unusual thing for her, but she liked it and hoped it would last. She just wanted to do everything to make him happy. Rose then wondered how Stella was taking the situation. Knowing well what she was like, and having experienced her vindictive side, Rose worried that it was nowhere near the happy ending that she'd read in the books. Rose knew in her heart that Stella would not just go out of their lives. What if she was never out of their lives? Oh, what a horrible thought that was.

The carriage came to a halt shaking Rose from her thoughts. She had been so wrapped up in thought that she hadn't realised that they had been so close Aunt Beatrice's house. The sun had gone down by now and the warm glow was gone, replaced by a blue grey hue making the air feel colder.

Once inside Aunt Beatrice hugged Rose and kissed her on the cheek like she was her own daughter.

'Good evening aunt. I hope you're well?'

'Oh yes, my dear. I trust you are well too?' Aunt Beatrice took Rose's arm, and they walked the long hallway to the large green room at the end of it. 'Now sit here, we must talk about the next plans.'

Aunt Beatrice was very touchy feely these days. Rose didn't mind, especially not from aunt. It was the opposite to how Louie had always described her. It was such a warming feeling to have people so close to her that she could class as family. She'd never really known hers.

They spent the evening talking about the colours and fabrics that they might use to finish the upstairs rooms and what furniture they might need. They drank lots of tea and at one point had an enormous piece of sponge cake. Usually, they would have strawberries too but it was getting a bit late in the season for strawberries now.

Aunt really was very good at decorating rooms and working out what needed to be done, and where it needed to be done. Her own house looked like a palace, every wall, corner and ceiling absolutely perfect. Everything from the pictures to the plants were flawlessly placed. This was why Rose encouraged Aunt Beatrice's input for the house. Rose herself wouldn't know where to start, she'd had the idea but taking it to fruition would have been a completely different story.

'One day it would be lovely to see you and Louie here together and we could really get things going.'

'I know aunt, he's rather busy today, but he's happy with everything.' Rose wondered what Aunt Beatrice thought of their seemingly odd relationship. She wondered if Louie had discussed it with his aunt. He always seemed so closed off from his aunt; he never opened up or told her everything. Rose couldn't understand that because she knew that aunt would do everything to help him.

'Not that ghastly Stella woman?' aunt pulled such a face of utter disgust that it made Rose smile.

'Actually yes, but he's hopefully getting her to move back in with her father. He's quite old and apparently near destitute since the larger alehouse opened. Anyway, hopefully we won't see her anymore.' That thought certainly made Rose smile.

'Good, it's about time. She's a money sponge. I'm sure she's trying to swindle my naïve nephew at every opportunity and succeeding.' with another look of disgust Rose watched aunt take a large mouthful of tea from one of the pretty cups adorned with hand painted flowers and gold rims.

Rose wondered about this. Louie had never mentioned anything like that to her but wondered if Stella was using him for money. It would make sense; she would know about the inheritance. Maybe that was the piece of the puzzle she was missing, the letters in the study, the money problems.

It was pitch black by the time that Rose got back in her carriage to go home again. She took the chance to think about the way that Louie had held her tight in his arms last night and how he had looked at her and kissed her earlier in the day. He had been so gentle and loving; she'd found it hard to believe. The day had cheered her up and she wasn't going to let those thoughts of Stella interrupt that happiness this time.

Rose loved the darkness, the night – she could look out of the carriage and look at whatever was in her mind's eye and whatever she wanted to daydream about.

The journey back didn't seem like it had taken long which was a bit of a shame because she was enjoying her thoughts, but on the other hand it was nice to be back, because now perhaps she could see Louie again and he would hold her again, and this time it would be real, rather than her imagination.

There was an extra carriage outside, but Rose thought nothing of it and went up to her private bedroom. Rose noticed there was a bit of a smell of smoke in the house but nothing seemed to be out of the ordinary, so she continued to the room. Perhaps the extra carriage was the chimney sweep. She wanted to freshen up before going to see Louie and finding out how his day went. Perhaps he hadn't even arrived back from taking Stella back home yet. She had briefly managed to forget that it was happening.

She was startled by a loud, aggressive knock on the door. Opening it she saw Louie and Elizabeth. Behind them was... *Stella!* Why was *she* still here? Either side of Stella were two policemen. What *is* going on?

The policemen pushed past Elizabeth and Louie taking hold of one of Rose's wrists. Thankfully it wasn't the one that had been burnt otherwise it would have been painful.

'We must take you to the station for questioning. You are being arrested for theft and arson. Come with us please.' Firmly, Rose was taken past everyone and through the house. Rose was terrified. She knew that she could be facing life in a prison for such a serious charge of arson, but how had all this come about?

That would explain the smell when she came home, and the extra carriage.

'Wait, Louie... what's happened? Why me?' The terror was growing in Rose faster than burning gunpowder.

'This way please, you can't talk to anyone at the moment until we've got your version of events.' The men tugged her to get her to continue walking towards the door. Stella had a horrible, nasty, evil grin that Rose thought she might remember for many years to come. What did they mean by, 'her version of events'?

'Louie!' Rose screamed. She looked at him and tried to go towards him holding her arms out but instead got pulled away. He looked as scared as she felt. Stella put her arm in his with a great big smile. Elizabeth was crying, Rose had never seen her sad, in fact she'd never seen her without a smile. The policemen tugged her even harder, and she had to turn around to face the direction that she was being dragged in – out of the door.

'Louuiiieee!'

Chapter thirteen

T he night had taken a turn that Rose had never expected, her life had a habit of doing that in the last few months. It was such a shock after having had a lovely and relaxing day. She still had no idea what had gone on at the house and why she was in this position. She had been sitting at a table in a small dusty room for what felt like an hour or more. There was nothing on any of the walls except for a large, plain, railway station type clock on one wall.

Two men finally came in, they were different ones to the ones that were at the house. One had a uniform on and the other wore just a normal suit. They sat at the table with Rose; the one in the suit looked as though he was going to be the one in charge.

'Please, could you tell me what's going on and what I'm being accused of?' Rose pleaded with the man in the suit. She thought he looked like his name would be John; John suited him.

'You can make this whole process a lot faster by just admitting it, making a statement and we can all go home.' He said looking sternly at her. Rose was taken aback. She thought that 'John' might have had more of a friendly nature.

'I don't even know what I'm supposed to be admitting to! I've been out most of the day and arrived back when you all came and knocked on my bedroom door!' Rose was feeling frustrated. The man looked up at the uniformed policeman and seemed like he'd been pushed off course a little.

'What time did you go out?' He asked.

'Gosh, I have no idea, I didn't look at the time. It was after breakfast and before lunch, that's all I know. I'd been with Louie for a while before I left so he might be able to tell you. All I know is

that the sun was starting to go down after I'd gone to the town and got in the carriage to go and see aunt.' Rose wondered why Louie hadn't already told them all of these details. .
'You made it look like you were going out. It's a big house – you can easily hide. Then, when you did go out you started trying to sell the things you'd taken.' He stopped talking as though waiting for a reaction. Rose realised her mouth was agape.
'Why would I do that? I still don't understand I'm afraid.'
'Who did you sell them to?' He demanded. 'When you went to the town, you sold the things you stole.'
'Sell *what* to?' Rose really wished that *'John'* would answer her and tell her what had happened properly.
'We found some of the items you stole, in *your* room. The rest of the things you intended to sell no doubt. There're still some items missing, and we will find them. Then there's the damage to everything else that was broken. The fire is of course more serious, you could have killed someone.' *'John'* really was making no sense.
'I have no idea what you're talking about. I got up after spending the night with Louie. He had some things to do, and I think that was when he would have spoken to Stella to tell her he was taking her home to her father tonight, then I saw Louie again and we spent some time together. Straight after that I left the house and went to town for a couple of errands and then to aunt's house where I spent the rest of the day, before coming home to this.' Rose was feeling very frustrated and angry, a little humiliated perhaps.
'John' slammed the desk with his hands before putting a pipe in his mouth. He looked as angry as she felt. He seemed sure that she had done something. The suited man stood up taking the pipe from his mouth, his grey hair flopping into his sweaty face and his nicotine-stained moustache twitching.
'We'll do this again tomorrow. You'll be in prison for the rest of your life, so perhaps you should think about your story overnight. We've got witnesses and you've already admitted going to town.'
The man and the policeman left the room, soon followed by another policeman who came into the room. Rose was escorted to a small, dark, cold cell. Rose was glad that Aunt Beatrice had given

her a warm scarf before she had left.

Rose didn't sleep; she was too cold apart from anything else. She went from sitting to pacing the small room and back again a hundred times. The night was possibly the longest night she had ever known. Although the brown blanket was rough, itchy and uncomfortable it did provide a good degree of warmth in the small dark hours, and she was grateful for it.

The confusion was the hardest thing. One minute she was having tea with Aunt Beatrice and the next she was here, tired and still with not really much of an idea what had gone on.

Eventually something beige and hot in a bowl arrived for her to eat. It was worse than workhouse food. She left it uneaten and wasn't particularly hungry anyway.

Suddenly the locks on the door were being noisily opened and to her great surprise, Aunt Beatrice came into the tiny, grubby cell. Rose had never been so happy to see a familiar face before. They hugged and Aunt Beatrice held Rose's hands in hers. It was still most unusual as aunt was not particularly tactile or outwardly affectionate other than the greetings and goodbyes where you would know that you were loved. The door had closed again and been re-bolted. The two women sat down; Beatrice was still holding Rose's hands. Rose felt sudden waves of emotion and began to feel hot tears rolling uncontrollably down her face. Beatrice looked intently into Rose's eyes as though she was trying to extract her very memories and thoughts.

'If I ask you some questions, will you tell me the truth Rose?'

'Of *course,* I have no reason to do anything else. I wish I knew what was going on.'

'They haven't told you?'

'No, not really. They've asked some questions and then repeated them and got cross because I didn't say the right thing.' Rose shrugged.

Beatrice sighed. 'Before you came to my house yesterday, did you do *anything* that you shouldn't have done?'

'No, why would I? But, like what? It was a normal day. When I got back I just went up to my room to freshen up from the day and was hoping I might see Louie. He was supposed to have taken Stella to her father by the evening,' Rose said earnestly, she really wished she knew what had happened.

'You didn't break anything in the main bedroom? Or steal any of the statuettes?'

Rose felt herself frowning. 'no. I didn't go anywhere near there; not until I got back - I'd gone to my own room to freshen up before I saw Louie, like I said. Why did it smell smoky? I'm being blamed for that too?'

'Some things had been burned yes, and yes – whoever broke the porcelain and stole the other items is the person that set fire to some things. Thankfully the fire was found before it took hold and was put out quite quickly. The trouble is Rose, that some of the missing items were found in one of your bags. It was by the door; you must have put it there when you came in. They think that you went out in the afternoon to go and sell the items. They'd found other things in your room earlier on.'

Rose thought for a moment. 'But I don't need money – Louie and Elizabeth keep us comfortable and in everything that we need .I've never had money and so I don't need it now. Anyway, I didn't bring a bag yesterday.'

This made Beatrice think. 'No, you didn't did you. Hmm. What about the fire, apparently you've done it before.'

Rose gasped in disbelief. Had Louie said these cruel things after he *knew* what had gone on that day? Rose pulled her sleeve up and showed aunt the full burn. It still wasn't healed and was painful. 'Stella did this. I did not start a fire or burn the book. I burned my hand rescuing the book because I knew how special it was to Louie. She had thrown all of my books into the fire.'

'What books Rose? And why do you say you've not had money before? Are you not from a rich family?'

'I'm from the workhouse.' Rose looked down embarrassed. Her entire world was crumbling, what would aunt think now? She would surely retract everything. What would happen to Louie once Beatrice knew everything. 'I have some deafness and so I never learned to read and write properly. Louie taught me everything. I taught him some sign language that I know. We taught each other. I loved being in the library and we would often spend time in there. Sometimes he would read some of those books to me, for hours. He taught me arithmetic, geography and so many other things. He's been such a good man and has changed my life. I don't think I could bear to go back to the workhouse now.' Rose was still looking down and hadn't dared to look up to see what expression Beatrice might have. Rose was sure she would be very angry right now.

'So, it's a marriage of convenience?' Said aunt. Oh no, thought Rose, now she would feel used and betrayed.

'It was, to start with. But now it's not. I think I love him Aunt Beatrice. We've been through so much and we've become closer every day, especially over the last couple of weeks. But whatever should happen now, and whatever becomes of me, please, *please* continue with the plans for the house, for Louie.'

Rose looked directly at Beatrice and aunt in turn stared intently back. Cupping Rose's face in her hands Beatrice nodded, reassuring Rose, 'I believe you. I shall go to the house and speak to Louie. I think this is all that Stella creature. I have no idea how we are ever going to prove it was her and not you but, I'm going to give it all I've got.' Rose felt tears escaping again, relieved that aunt wasn't going to brush her off now she knew where she'd come from.

With no time to waste Beatrice stood up, bending back down to kiss Rose on the forehead before knocking on the door, indicating to the guard that she was finished and ready to leave.

'Try not to worry. We'll get to the bottom of this.'

The door slammed closed again echoing around the small cell before silence hit Rose's ears as if there'd never been anyone there.

Chapter fourteen

L ouie quietly slid out of the bed. He couldn't sleep. Once out of bed he threw a gown over his naked body and looked back at the bed where Stella lay, blissfully asleep. He felt angry at himself because he'd let her in again. The alcohol hadn't helped. She'd encouraged him but he knew he couldn't keep blaming her for his actions. His confusion and doubt about Rose had played havoc with his emotions and Stella had managed to take full advantage of that.

Again.

He didn't even like this room, it always felt so.... dirty. Now he felt dirty too. At least he hadn't been able to give Stella what she really wanted. He laughed to himself because she had tried so hard. But it just hadn't felt right, and he was unable to 'get in the mood'. He was also still immensely worried that she would have a baby and he would be stuck forever. The worry increased through time.

He quietly left the room so as not to wake Stella and went to one of the small bathrooms on the upper floors so that he could not be found if she should wake up. He washed his face in cold water making him gasp. The rooms up here were already cold in the early Autumn hours and the fires were never lit up here. He washed his entire body slowly and methodically, attempting to wash all trace of Stella away. His head hurt as he'd drunk far too much last night. He hadn't had a drink like that since paying the alehouse off.

After washing several times, he went to his special room. There were still ornaments smashed and ripped books from the day before. Louie felt a deep sadness washing over him, like he was mourning his parents all over again. They would have been devastated to see this room like this. He found some clean and fresh clothes that hadn't been ripped or slashed and put them on. Somehow, he still felt disgusted with himself.

Slowly he went down the flights of stairs and started towards his study. Before he could get there his Aunt Beatrice appeared at the front door. Letting herself in and without any words they both made their way to the study together.

Louie perched on the front of his desk feeling too restless to walk around and sit in the chair. Aunt watched his face and went to him. She kissed his cheek and rubbed his face with her gloved hand. It was an unusual amount of affection from her to him Louie thought. She was usually quite brash with him and impatient. He mulled over his life choices and realised that he probably made her like that. She was probably constantly exasperated with him. He'd managed to prove his stupid decision-making capabilities, or lack of them, last night.

'I'm sorry Aunt Beatrice, I've lied to you and kept things from you.' Louie was feeling quite sad today and he couldn't see how anything could improve that feeling. He had never quite felt this low, certainly not to the extent that he had no idea what to do for the best about anything. He felt like there wasn't even anything to look forward to anymore.

Anywhere.

With anyone.

He missed Rose immensely, it was like a part of him was gone. He'd never felt this way, never missed anyone in quite the same way.

'I've been to see Rose this morning.' aunt said casually. Louie looked up at her in surprise.

'You did? How is she?'

'Well, she's sitting in a cold cell with no idea what is going on or why she is there. She's told me everything Louie, why didn't you tell me?' Beatrice's tone was much softer than usual. Louie shrugged. Why *hadn't* he?

'I don't know aunt; I suppose I was afraid of what you might do if you found out the truth.' Aunt Beatrice sighed noisily in exasperation.

'I would have helped you silly boy, I would have respected the honesty. The Will says nothing about the type of marriage, it only said you needed to be married. As it is you seem to have both become quite fond of each other. The real issue is Stella, what is going on with her?'

'I found out she's been blackmailing me. I paid her father at the alehouse. She said the amount had gone up and she was going to take it from me and pass it to her father – then I went to see her father and he was starving and near destitution.'

'That doesn't surprise me in the slightest. She's practically a whore. I don't know why you didn't see through her years ago. Anyway, the point is, we need to find out what went on yesterday; now, I've spoken to Rose and she's always been frightfully honest; so I have a sneaking suspicion that it was Stella who caused all the trouble last night and not Rose. We just need to prove that.'

'How in the world are we going to manage that?'

Aunt stared blankly at Louie, and he knew she had no idea either.

'Let's start by looking around the house.' Aunt Beatrice was already off marching towards the door before turning back to Louie impatiently. 'Well, come on.'

'Stella is still in the house aunt.' Louie reminded her.

'Pfft! I'm not worried about that!'

Oh gosh, thought Louie. A showdown between his aunt and Stella; that would not end well. Louie jumped up from the desk following his aunt out of the study wondering, and worried about what she might do next.

Elizabeth was in the main entrance hall and looked up to see what the commotion was about.

'Have you seen Stella this morning Elizabeth?' Louie asked, both of them stopping in front of her.

The cook, looking less jolly than usual gestured towards the kitchen. 'She's in there, that's why I'm out here.' She said with an eye roll.

'Brilliant, keep her there!' aunt said, rushing up the first flight of stairs again before she'd even finished her sentence.

Aunt went towards his special room, but Louie was certain there was nothing new to see or find in there. They needed to check the other bedroom. 'This way, the other room.'

Aunt Beatrice looked at him bewildered. 'I never took her in there, not with me. We used another room, up the hall.' Louie walked past her taking her hand and leading her to the 'other room'. Once inside aunt began looking around and searching things that might belong to Stella for any clues.

'Louie, look under the bed. I'm going to check through the clothes.' Beatrice started pulling clothes and bags at random checking pockets.

'Aunt even if we find something she could lie and say we put it there.'

'I've thought of that, we'll just keep her out. Don't touch anything we find and call the police back.'

'Wait, aunt, I've found something.' He pulled a bag out from under the bed. It was a pretty bag with lace and pastel fabrics. It wasn't Stella's style at all. Far too pretty. 'This looks like it might be Rose's bag.'

Beatrice came over to inspect the find. Inside the bag they found more items from inside the special room. Things of great value and a large amount of money were stuffed inside the tiny bag. There were items of his Mum's jewellery that his father had kept all through the years.

'Is it definitely Rose's bag?' Asked Beatrice. Digging a little deeper they found a small purse. The purse itself was empty, but inside was embroidered the name, 'Rose'.

'Rose has never been in this room, I'm certain.' Louie said excitedly to Beatrice. This was it, it's what they needed. Proof that it was actually Stella.

'Now comes the difficult bit. We have to get the police to listen. Maybe it would help if we could do a timeline of her movements yesterday and maybe even see if there's anyone that might have seen Stella. They look very different so I'm sure someone must have noticed.'

They pushed the bag back in and quietly locked the hallway door that led to the kitchen, giving the key to Elizabeth. Stella wouldn't be able to get out because Elizabeth had already locked the back door and had the key firmly in her apron. Elizabeth smiled at the growing collection of keys and the thought that Stella was being held captive, even if it was in her beloved kitchen.

'We need a plan. I'll go to the police station. Aunt, why don't you see if you can find out about Rose's movements and Elizabeth, see if you can find anyone that saw Stella or saw her trying to sell anything.'

The three left the large house leaving Stella locked in the kitchens currently unaware of the locked doors or of what was going on around her.

The house was silent when the police officer knocked on the door, hoping that someone would be in.

Chapter fifteen

'**H**as anyone come for me?' Rose asked hopefully. 'John' was a little more amenable now, but Rose still disliked him for the way that he had spoken to her previously and assumed her guilt.

'No, no-one. Were you expecting someone?'

'Oh erm, no, not really.' She replied quietly. Inside her head was much less quiet. It was filled with thoughts like, why wasn't Louie here to meet her, or Aunt Beatrice? Did she mean so little to everyone? Had something else happened? The policeman earlier had said he would go to the house and tell everyone what had happened.

Outside the station it was raining, hard. The cobbles were shiny, and the birds were hiding in the safety of the trees. Looking around she still couldn't see any sign of a familiar face. She wondered what to do. Rose knew that a decision had to be made right now. She began to walk, at first not really knowing where she was going to go, and not really caring either at this point. She was free, but what was the cost of that freedom? She had tried so hard over the last few months for Louie and the family, but Stella always won over. Rose felt she just couldn't do it anymore. She'd been through enough and had the scars to prove it. At least she could read and write now so maybe some opportunities might come up, or perhaps she would have to go back to the workhouse where she had come from. But the whole world was a different place now and her time there seemed like a surreal part of her life that had never happened.

Maybe she could go and stay at Aunt Beatrice's house. Maybe she wouldn't be able to call her aunt anymore. She felt suddenly angry as her thoughts turned to Louie and the previous night. Why had he allowed Stella to stay? The only reason that Rose could think of, as to why he hadn't taken Stella back to the alehouse and her father, was because Louie had believed that Rose was capable of damaging all of his parents' lovely things, that he cherished. This hurt a lot. Deep down. How could anyone think that of her, and after all she had tried to do for Louie and the house, and everything that she thought they'd had together.

The rain became harder and was bouncing off itself back into the air. She knew she would be soaked in no time. She hurried down a small alley where there was a little shelter from the buildings and she stayed there for a while. She stood looking out onto the main road where horses came sloshing through the growing puddles and people hurried from one place to another. Rose had taken no money; wherever she went from here she would have to walk. She was beginning to shiver as some of her clothes were beginning to let the rain through already.

It would take several hours, but Aunt Beatrice's house would be the safest bet she thought. She was sure that Beatrice would at least give her somewhere to sleep. Maybe she would take her on as staff, a maid or something. It would all depend on what Louie might have said to her, but she'd got a good impression when Beatrice had visited her in the cell. She only hoped that nothing had changed in the meantime.

The rain didn't let up. As if things couldn't get any worse a thunderstorm also began rumbling around in the sky. Rose noticed that the bottom of her dress was covered in mud and various splatters from walking and where carriages had gone past. A couple of small tears had appeared in the lower fabric.

Progressively Rose became colder and colder to the point where she couldn't control the shivering. Her clothes were saturated all the way through to her skin, and so were not only giving her no protection from the weather but were also incredibly heavy, making the walk even slower.

Rose had no idea what the time was, or how long she had been walking for, but it had been dark for a very long time when she arrived at Aunt Beatrice's house. The walk from the main gate to the front door seemed almost as long as the entire days walk.

Rose's mind was blank. She had thought so many things that she didn't have the power to think any more. Every now and then she would begin crying uncontrollably all over again. The world was once again a completely different place, more hostile and without love. Shivering, she finally reached the front porch and dragged herself up the steps, stumbling on her now ragged and ripped dress, crawling up them on all fours.

Rose didn't even have the power or the want to knock on the door. She turned her back to it and slumped against it, hugging her legs into herself as tightly as she could and lowering her head into her knees. At least she didn't have to walk any more. Still crying for the umpteenth time that day, she couldn't see anything through her blurry vision. Rose began to feel disorientated and didn't really know where she was any more. Maybe she would fall asleep. Maybe she would wake up in this same position. Or maybe she would wake up in the warmth and softness of the special room and Louie would be there, holding her tightly, telling her how much he loved her. Then this would all have just been a terrible, terrible dream and everything would be all right.

The wind blew her already tangled mop of hair making her feel even colder. It was a cold she'd never felt, even in the depths of winter in the workhouse when the inmates would huddle for warmth.

Chapter sixteen

L ouie looked at his aunt confused and then back to the police sergeant. 'What do you mean she's not here?'

'Exactly that, she left hours ago, went that way.' the man waggled a finger in the general direction that Rose might have gone although Louie felt suspicious of how much notice the man had actually taken of her as he didn't seem interested in much at all. 'We released her. We had to. Someone came in and gave a statement to say his daughter had been seen selling some of the items. We did send an officer to your house but perhaps you missed him.'

'What!?' Louie's eyes lit up and his heart skipped a beat. Aunt Beatrice grabbed Louie's arm in shock. Louie turned to his aunt again. 'It must have been Stella's dad! Goodness.'

'Do you know where this Stella is then Sir?' Asked the policeman who seemed to have suddenly perked up.

Squeezing his arm even harder than she already was, Beatrice gasped. 'She's still in the kitchen!' They had half forgotten about her as it had been a long day and they had been concentrating on getting Rose out of the cell.

'Take me there.' The policeman had suddenly come alive and called out for two of his colleagues to go with him.

They all got into a large carriage, although it was still a bit of a squeeze. The rain had made all of their clothes smell so the carriage had a strong, almost unbearable odour. It didn't take long to reach Louie's house though.

The thunderstorm was lighting up the small track to the house as it was now almost completely dark. It was barely four in the afternoon and almost pitch black. All of them alighted the carriage and went into the house going towards the kitchen with Louie and Aunt Beatrice leading the small group of police officers. They were joined near the stairs by Elizabeth.

'Sorry Sir, I had to come back – I was soaked through!' Louie looked at Elizabeth's bright red cheeks still cold from outside and kissed her on the cheek.

'It's all right Elizabeth, Rose has been released. Stella is being arrested.' Louie looked around frowning. 'Has Rose come back?'

The cook made a disappointed face and shook her head. 'Not that I know of.'

'The kitchen?' piped in a voice from behind them. It was the main police officer who had gone from disinterested to impatient.

Elizabeth retrieved the key and let everyone in. Stella smiled an evil smile. She was standing against the sink on the other side of the kitchen, leaning on her hands that were behind her back.

The police officers began to walk towards her with the intention of making the arrest.

'Wait!' shouted Stella. From behind her back, she retrieved one of the largest meat cleavers that Elizabeth owned. Aunt gasped as did Elizabeth.

'Now come on, you don't want to do that Stella.' Said one of the uniformed policemen. 'Let's just put that down and quietly come with us and get this all over and done with.' He remained calm and held a hand out towards Stella. She looked at him with utter disgust.

'It'll never be over and done with.' Stella said turning abruptly towards Louie and lunging towards his chest with the cleaver in a chopping motion. Louie jumped backwards knocking into Aunt Beatrice who had screamed.

'There's actually something wrong with you Stella. Please accept what is happening, you are finally going to pay the consequences of your actions. Leave me alone, *please*, let our family be in peace.' Louie pleaded with Stella. Her eyes were sparkling, and she was still grinning, enjoying the moment.

'I'll never leave your family in peace. You have no idea, do you?'

'What are you talking about Stella, you're making no sense.' said

Louie. Stella laughed.

'Your father ruined my father. He would have the biggest alehouse in the country. We would have had everything Louie. So, you see, I'm just taking what should have been mine to start with! And there's no way that the stupid floor scrubber is going to take that place.' Her eyes were big, and her teeth gritted. Stella was red with anger. Louie was taken aback and had no idea what to say. He'd known little of his father's business dealings and would never really know what had gone on in that situation because he wasn't here to ask. Suddenly Stella lunged again. Louie jumped back again pushing aunt into Elizabeth. Stella had misjudged her lunge and fell into the large table in the centre of the kitchen catching the cleaver in such a way that as it fell, she accidentally chopped the end of two of her fingers completely off. Stella screamed a blood curdling scream. The police took the unexpected opportunity to snatch the knife from her and get her restrained. Beatrice had sat on the floor feeling faint and Louie stumbled backwards feeling a little sick.

Stella was taken out of the house briskly by the police officers who Louie thought had proved themselves in the end to be quite efficient. Louie felt hot, lost and agitated. This was not how he ever envisaged the end of his odd relationship with Stella. He realised that Elizabeth and Beatrice had just witnessed a most awful accident and immediately went to comfort them, leading them out of the kitchen and into the drawing room. He sat them both down and made sure the fire was well alight before going back to the kitchen to fetch tea. As he reached the kitchen the incident flashed before his eyes, and he felt nauseous and a little faint again. But this was his house and he was going to have to get those memories erased from his mind.

Returning to the front room he found Beatrice and Elizabeth being comforted by the policeman that had earlier seemed less interested. The policeman stood up and shook Louie's hand once he'd put the tea tray on the table.

'Rest assured, she'll do a lot of years, probably in the asylum, she might never get out after tonight.' With that, the policeman bid his goodnight individually to the ladies and then to Louie and left. Louie had so many thoughts and emotions right now. He didn't know what to think or feel.

'I'll get you a carriage aunt, you should go home and rest. We'll talk things over tomorrow.'

'Would you want to stay here tonight, Louie? After all that has happened? Why don't you come and stay with me for a few weeks, heaven knows there's enough rooms? Elizabeth can come too. We'll spend some time then cleaning up and sorting this house out. How *you* want it. For you and Rose.'

Louie thought that was a good idea. He didn't really want to stay here and see that room. Or even his room, empty without Rose in it. Louie looked at his aunt. 'But where is Rose?'

'She'll turn up. Come, it's a journey in this weather. Let's get to my house into some warmth.'

The couple of hour trip seemed to drag even more than usual but Louie felt glad to have got away from the house. It didn't feel homely anymore. It felt evil and wretched. He wondered if he'd ever want to go back. Oh the irony, of the inheritance, and now he wasn't sure he ever wanted to step foot in the door again.

The rough cold journey eventually came to an end. Inside aunt's house it felt warm. It was a long time since he'd actually stayed overnight here. He was a child last time that happened. Inside he felt a little excited, almost in a childlike manner, to be able to stay in this house, so much more grand than his own, with his aunt again.

Louie was shown his room, and everyone said good night, not wanting to spend any more time within this day than they had already. The door closed; Louie looked around the room. It had a familiar aroma that he always associated with his aunt. It made him feel warm inside. In the centre of the large room was an enormous four poster bed. He studied the fabrics and felt the wood carvings before holding tightly onto one of the ornate posts and leaning into it, finally able to let out all of his emotions of the day, of the year.

He had no idea how long he cried for, but he knew it was a

long time. The candle that had been by the side of the bed had burnt out and he had a painful head. He wanted to hold Rose. He knew he had made a huge mistake by not taking Stella back to her father that night regardless of what had happened and what she had claimed. Rose probably thought he detested her. *She* probably detested him, and who would blame her. He'd always trusted Stella's word over Rose's simply because Rose was from the workhouse and because he'd known Stella all his life. He thought about how stupidly crazy this was. Rose was honest, he *knew* that. Why hadn't he stuck up for Rose more?

His thoughts then turned to the atlas. He remembered he hadn't stuck up for Rose then either, even when he knew that Stella had lied. He pulled and squeezed his hair while thinking about this in frustration. He kept asking himself, why?

He'd had the love of the most generous and beautiful soul right there in front of him and he'd kept turning to Stella. Louie began punching the softness of the bed. He was enraged with himself and kept punching it until his breath and strength had run out. Louie lay on the bed where he had been punching, calming his breathing and feeling suddenly overwhelmed with tiredness. The rain pitter- pattered on the window. The wind had come up and howled around the bay window. Every now and then the wind would make the rain hit the window harder leading to an ebb and flow of rain sounds which Louie found quite calming and comforting.

Chapter seventeen

L ouie awoke to a great commotion somewhere in the house. He didn't remember falling asleep and was still in much the same position and fully clothed. He knew he looked a mess but felt he needed to go and find out what was going on.

Brushing his fingers through his hair he rushed out of the bedroom door and raced down the stairs towards the noises of the maids, butler and females of the house. The main grand staircase that led from the first to ground floor opened gracefully onto a large entrance hall. From there was the large front door and ornate porch that distinguished this house from the others in the village. Louie could see from the top of the last flight, the door wide open and everyone crowding but he didn't know what they were crowding around.

As he got closer, he could see the shape of a person on the floor, it was a lady ; yes, there were lots of skirts even if they were in tatters.

Aunt Beatrice had noticed him at the last minute and jumped up to stop Louie getting too close before he knew who it was. 'It's Rose! She's barely alive, we must fetch the doctor!'

Louie was shocked. This was not how he wanted today to start, and he felt huge guilt. This was his fault. He bent down and gently picked her up in his arms, her legs and the still wet dress draped over one arm and her head cradled between his chest and elbow the other side.

'This way' Beatrice said hurrying in front of him. 'Elizabeth, please go and fetch the doctor.'

They went back up the stairs and to a room on the first floor. Beatrice opened the door onto an enormous bedroom with two large sets of bay windows. They could see the dust floating in the rays of sunlight streaming in through the windows.

Louie knelt on the large bed so that he could put Rose carefully down. Beatrice ushered him out of the room quickly. 'We need to get her out of these wet clothes immediately.'

Outside the room Louie paced around the large corridor. The theme of the downstairs rooms continued up here. There was carpeting covered in thick pile rugs. On the walls were dozens of paintings above which was a shelf that ran the entire length of the corridor. On this were plants, some hanging and some with flowers. Everything was perfectly in place as with everywhere else in the house. He'd never known his aunt to live any differently.

Elizabeth arrived and came up the stairs with the doctor. She was breathless from running and slumped in a chair that was placed against a wall in the corridor near the top of the stairs.

'You're an angel Elizabeth. Thank you so much.' He knew she worked so hard for everything that she did. Sometimes he felt sorry for her that she didn't have a husband, but she seemed quite happy with whatever her relationship was with the doctor.

'I'm sure she'll be fine sir.' Elizabeth tried to reassure him, but he could hear the doubt in her own voice. The door opened and both Louie and Elizabeth stiffened wondering what the news would be. Aunt Beatrice closed the door quietly. Louie's heart began to race, he couldn't help but think the worst possible scenario. Beatrice turned to face them. Louie's heart pounded even harder.

'The doctor says she's probably been outside all night, at least. She has hypothermia and may have got a fever from being wet and cold all night. If only we'd known she was there.' Aunt looked down. Louie wondered if she was feeling guilty too, not that she had a reason. At least Rose was still alive.

'He said he's not sure how long it will take for Rose to recover, or if she will fully. We'll have to see.'

Louie felt his heart sink a little. Beatrice came to stand next to him and rubbed his arm. 'It'll be all right Louie; we'll look after her.'

He began pacing again waiting for the doctor to come out. Louie ran his hands through his hair and rubbed his face, now quite itchy and prickly from having not shaved for a couple of days.

Finally, the doctor came quietly out of the room. Aunt Beatrice greeted him, and he gave her a couple of bottles of medicine.

'Give her this one with lemon and honey four times a day, and this one at night. Keep her warm and don't make her do too much or cause stress. She needs to rest. I'll come and see her tomorrow, about this time.'

The doctor left, gliding down the stairs quietly.

'Can I see her, aunt?' It's all Louie wanted in the entire world.

'Yes, of course. Remember what the doctor said. It's going to take time.'

Louie wasn't sure if he had time. He knew Rose probably hated him now. He'd never supported her, certainly not enough or in the way his father would have done with his mother.

Something was stopping him going into the room. He didn't want to see her ill or unhappy.

'Well, what are you waiting for?' aunt said making him jump out of his thoughts.

'I don't really know. What if she doesn't want to see me?'

'Well then you cross that bridge when we get there. Be gentle, it won't last. She loves you too much.'

Louie looked inquisitively at his aunt wondering how she had deducted that? Had Rose said something?

Slowly he got his legs working and approached the room. His heart began thumping hard again. He was excited to see her but incredibly nervous at the same time.

Louie was a little grateful that Rose was asleep when he went in. He sat next to her on the bed wanting to kiss her gently on the head or hold her hand. But it didn't feel right, like he should. Not at the moment anyway.

Rose slept most of that first day and Louie refused to leave her side even though she didn't seem happy to see him on the occasions that she woke up. She'd seemed confused, and would turn her back to him, but he refused to leave or to think that they could be apart for the rest of their lives. Even though his neck hurt from sitting in awkward positions, Louie couldn't bear the thought of leaving her on her own overnight. Look what happened the last time he did that. He'd already decided he would never do that again. So, he pulled up a chair next to the bed and slept resting his head on the bed near Rose and sitting beside the bed, in the uncomfortable, hard chair.

They both woke a few times during the night, one would stir and wake the other up. No words were exchanged. Louie would just watch her. She looked so different to when he'd met her. Her face was so pure it made him feel at peace.

Several days passed without too much difference. Louie would change position from the chair to the bed side to the window and back to the chair. He hardly left the room, only when he really needed to. He had begun reading to her. There were some legends and myths in the library here, and he knew that she had enjoyed reading them in their lessons at home. He enjoyed reading to Rose and did so from his many positions around the room. Every now and then Elizabeth would come in and bring him food or tea although he hadn't eaten much as he didn't feel like it.

When he wasn't reading, he'd become so accustomed to talking to the air that he started to have conversations with her. He would tell her what it was like outside, whether it was cold or anything that had gone on in the house, like the new maid breaking one of aunt's favourite tea pots.

Every now and then he would say 'Please wake up properly, soon, my beautiful Rose.'

Aunt would bring the medication and stay for a while. She would make Louie go and get cleaned up and get some fresh air because she 'didn't want him ill too!'

Louie was beginning to wonder if Rose was ever going to wake up properly. Would life ever be normal again he wondered? It became a routine, a habit, each day, medicine, breakfast, wash and a walk around the grounds, reading to Rose, reading another book, more medicine, sleeping awkwardly by the side of the bed.......

Chapter eighteen

Each time Rose opened her eyes everything was a bit blurry and strange. She didn't know where she was or how she got there. Louie was always there. She wasn't sure she wanted him there, after all he'd never been there for her before. Her mind would wander and feel bad for thinking such thoughts, he'd helped her read and write for a start. Then her mind would blur with her eyes, or she'd feel so overwhelmingly sad that she would close her eyes again and go back to sleep. At least in that world no one could hurt her or accuse her of anything.

Rose had no idea what day it was but knew it had been dark several times. Sometimes at night she would wake and find Louie asleep with his head next to her. He would be sat on the uncomfortable chair and slumped equally uncomfortably over the bed. Rose wondered why he never slept next to her on the bed instead of sitting in the chair, or even why he seemed to stay in the room all of the time. At night he would sleep so deeply that he wouldn't feel Rose stroke his hair as he slept. He wouldn't notice her rubbing her fingers around his face feeling every lump, bump, and hair. His skin was soft she noticed. There would usually be a book near his hand, and she thought he might have been reading out loud.

Sometimes when Louie's hand was there Rose would gently rub each individual finger and thumb. He wouldn't wake from his sleep, and she wondered why he was so tired.

As the days passed and her thoughts became clearer, Rose started to think about things more. Her mind and heart felt torn. On one side she didn't want to go back to the workhouse, it was a different world now. She couldn't just leave this house, wherever it was, because she had no money and no way of living somewhere or getting work. She wasn't sure that she could forgive Louie for those last days that she remembered. It had hurt, really hurt. More so that Stella had still been there, she still didn't understand why he hadn't taken her back regardless of the situation. On the other side, she knew that Louie and herself had shared something quite special. Not just intimately, but in all the other times when they were together and when they weren't. But now she wondered if she'd just imagined all of that.

While Louie slept Rose would look around. It wasn't a room she'd seen before, but it was similar in style to Aunt Beatrice's house. Suddenly she remembered the night when she'd been all wet and cold. She *had* come to Beatrice's, even though she hadn't had a chance to knock on the door. Perhaps she was still there?

Louie began to stir next to her. She wanted to pretend she was still asleep again but knew that she couldn't not speak to him for ever. He sat up on his elbows rubbing his eyes before looking directly at Rose and jumping because he wasn't expecting her to be awake and looking at him. He sat up straighter. Rose didn't know what to say to him and he wasn't saying anything to her either.

Rose couldn't take her gaze away. The little early morning light that was coming through the windows was lighting up his blue eyes. How could he look at her with such softness, love and affection and yet not trust her actions? She wondered what Louie was thinking.

Louie opened his mouth a couple of times like he was going to say something but then closed it again without uttering a word. All of the time their eyes stayed locked. He got up out of the chair and sat next to Rose on the bed, only looking away briefly to see where her hand was.

Looking back to her, his eyes sparkling in the sunrise, his fingers found her fingers and they began rubbing and intertwining them. Rose felt more confused than ever and looked away pulling her hand back. Looking back at Louie she could see the devastation spreading over his face. Was she making a mistake, she thought? Louie looked down at his hands which were now resting in his lap. His hair was bouncing in his eyes like she remembered it doing the first day, when he was getting everything ready to teach her the first things about reading and writing.

Rose wasn't showing it in her face but inside her head was a cacophony of thoughts. Maybe they could put the past behind them, maybe what they had was strong enough to get them through. Then in a flash she remembered Stella. The person who had nearly destroyed every single person around including Rose herself.

'Where is Stella?' Rose said finally. She had to know. Rose just had to know that she was out of their lives forever because she knew she couldn't deal with another adventure with her.

'She'll be in prison for a long time Rose. She might even be sent to the asylum yet, they haven't decided. When she comes out, she is not allowed near any of the houses. In fact, I don't think she'll even come back to the village. You know her father turned her in?'

Rose was stunned. 'Her own father?'

'He had nothing to lose. She'd left him destitute. She'd stolen from the alehouse too, for many years it seems.'

Rose chewed over this new information in her mind as the room became silent again. The light coming in the room now was a lovely shade of pink, as if it might snow. Rose looked up at Louie again and sure enough he was watching her.

'Rose, I'm *so* sorry. I've always been so wrapped up in my own life and plan that it had made me selfish to everyone else. You. You who have given me so much. You've made me and the house into what could be a wonderful business for us, and all the while I kept going back to what I knew.' He shuffled around a bit on the bed, nervously taking her hand again. 'I, I, I should never have...I don't know, I just never expected *this.* The day I took you from the workhouse I looked at you and thought... well it doesn't matter what I thought because yet again I was wrong. You are surrounded by such calm. Love. I love you Rose, and I couldn't bear to be without you. The last few weeks, I've stayed by your side as a promise to you that I'll never leave you again. I've been punished and tormented by my thoughts the whole time. You probably hate me with every bone in your body now. You probably can't see a

future with me.'
Rose had noticed his eyes were becoming more watery. He said weeks, she thought, had it really been that long? Here in this bed? He really had been dedicated. With Stella gone maybe she could give him another chance. Maybe this could work after all. Yet she still felt so incredibly sad. They'd been through so much and very little of it was pleasant. What if she was always sad?

Rose wiped away a tear that had just breached his eye and thought that he must be very sad too. The touch made him look into her eyes again. This time Rose let him rub her fingers around in his. It was lovely to feel his touch again. He put the other arm under hers and around her pulling them closer together. Rose knew those old feelings were coming back again. Maybe that was all that mattered. Slowly their bodies became closer. Rose could feel Louie's deep breaths on her cheek.

Outside the pinky grey colour shrouded the earth like a cloak, finally releasing the first large flakes of snow of this year.

Chapter nineteen

I t had taken another three and half months for Rose to be able to walk around the house a little and begin to do things. Louie had taken care of her every single day and Rose felt that their love was so deep that nothing and nobody could break it. Louie had attended her every need and had continued reading to her daily. She had really enjoyed this. It would bring back memories in the library when sometimes they would sit a little too close together and she would rest her head on his shoulder.

Rose had helped Aunt Beatrice with the plans for their house renovation for short periods in the afternoons when she was feeling stronger.

Louie had told Rose that he wanted to make the house theirs now. He would keep an area where he could remember his parents as he wished, but most of their belongings had been damaged, burnt or stolen, so there hadn't been much left. They had all stayed with Aunt Beatrice the entire time because none of them could face the house again in the same way that they had left it. The memories were too unbearable.

Rose hadn't needed to wish for anything, Beatrice paid for everything that needed to be done in the house.

One particularly snowy day in late February when they were unable to do anything in the house, Rose, Louie and Aunt Beatrice were sat in the large lounge with the fire blazing high, Rose had noticed that Louie had been very restless.

'Sit down boy, you're making my head spin.' Said Aunt Beatrice, making Rose giggle. She had no idea why he kept pacing the room and looking out of the window.

'Ah, finally – in a moment aunt, it's here!' Rose looked at Louie and then at Beatrice. She obviously was well aware of what Louie was referring to as she clapped her hands together, beaming an enormous smile, seemingly in excitement.

They couldn't hear the conversation going on in the hall unfortunately, so Rose was none the wiser.

'What's he up to aunt?' Beatrice just smiled and winked before returning to her embroidery which Rose knew bored aunt to tears, so she wondered if she was doing it just for the warmth of the large piece of fabric on her lap.

Rose felt nervous. Whatever was going on felt weirdly like it was all about her.

Finally, Louie came back in the room with the most enormous box which he set down onto the large coffee table which was usually adorned with some kind of cake. Rose had rather missed the cake today.

Louie came and sat in front of where Rose was sat, in the large armchair. He took her hands gently in his and looked earnestly at her.

'Rose... well, um.... I don't really know what to say or how to do this.'

Rose smiled, more out of confusion than anything else. Louie wasn't very good at talking about his feelings and usually ended up rambling which she was used to. She was just surprised that he was doing this in front of his aunt.

'We've been through so much this past year. I... we...we've got to know each other really well, in a way I never expected. You've changed my perception on life and about love. We're already married, but... well you deserve so much more... I want to give you so much more, so... well, I want to know if you wouldn't mind doing it all again, but this time we'll do it properly and there'll be lots of people and a big ball and wonderful food, all you can eat and more.'

Rose was too taken aback to say anything. Louie was shuffling around in his position so that he was sitting on one knee and had got something out of his trouser pocket.

'Rose, please will you marry me... again... properly... and this time,

I'd like us to be engaged... and I'd like you to have this... it was my mother's engagement ring that father gave her... it's the only one, he had it made for her when he was on one of his long trips away. What do you say Rose, I don't want to ever be apart, we can do anything.'

Louie's entire being was pleading with her. Rose didn't have to think for very long. Since she'd been feeling better, she had realised that they didn't need to ask or answer questions about what had already been and couldn't be changed. They had an understanding, from the way they looked at each other to the way they touched.

'Oh, yes, of course!'

Louie put the ring on her finger before giving her a kiss. Rose had forgotten that aunt was in the room and looked over to her to see her drying her eyes with a small pretty handkerchief while beaming with happiness.

'And this time you shall have a proper dress too...' Louie got up, still holding Rose's hand so that she got up with him. They went to the table, and he gestured her excitedly to open the box.

Louie always knew how to surprise her! Rose looked inside the box to see a white lacy dress.

'And this, was mine – we had it taken away to have it cleaned and repaired. It is also the only one that was made.' said aunt proudly.

They all pulled the beautiful white dress out of the box. It had intricate designs all over.

'Oh, it's *beautiful*.' Rose had never seen such an expensive, exquisite dress and never thought she'd get to wear one.

'And!' interrupted Louie 'that's not all.' Oh goodness, Rose wasn't sure she could take any more surprises.

'After the wedding, we will be able to move back to *our* house and it's all set to have people stay. Elizabeth will come back with us, and we will have some more maids.'

Louie was still smiling but Rose knew that her smile had slid down and was now more of an agape stare. She had got so used to being at Aunt Beatrice's, and the other house had so many horrible memories, that she'd never even thought about actually going back there.

Louie gently held the top of her arms. 'You won't recognise it, I promise. It's all changed. I didn't want those memories either.'

Rose felt relieved that he'd obviously had the same thoughts. They were always in the same place without even having to say anything. It was that understanding thing again. He knew what to say and when to say it.

There was nothing more perfect than what her life had finally become. Sometimes Rose even thought that the heartache to get there was worth it.

'There's even a mini library in our bedroom. And comfortable chairs so that I can always read to you, my love. And, next to our room.... I thought I might put a little nursery....' He said tentatively.

Rose smiled, and cried, and smiled some more.

'Now we can begin a new story, Rose. The story of Mr and Mrs King, and it will *always* have a happy ending.'

Books By This Author

Brimhaven

A historical romance of two people attempting to carve out new lives and both having to hide their pasts to try to achieve it. Florence has run away from her old life and wants to do something unexpected of women - she wants a career. Albert falls into his business after finding work at the local workhouse. But, then a face from the past turns up. Florence had once been betrothed to Henry, and he has no plans to lose his inheritance plan. Between Henry, father, and the lies and social expectations - can Albert ever win Florence over?

With Love x

Thank you for reading my book, I hope you
have enjoyed the journey.
Please follow me on Amazon and social media.

If you enjoyed the read, please leave a review.

Thank you so much, for supporting an independent writer.

Printed in Great Britain
by Amazon